Parastoo

Stories and Poems

Mehri Yalfani

women's
PRESS

CANADIAN CATALOGUING IN PUBLICATION DATA

Yalfani, Mehri.

 Parastoo

(International connections : women writers from around the world)
ISBN 0-88961-211-0
I. Title II. Series
PS8597.A54P3 1995   C813.54   C95-931881-X
PR9199.3.Y35P3 1995

"In Limbo," "Newcomer," "The First Day Without Home" (as "The First Day") and "In An Unknown House" (as "The Second Day") were previously published in *Fireweed* 44/45 (1994).

Editor: Rivanne Sandler
Copy editor: Nancy Chong
Proofreader: Sandra Haar
Cover illustration: Shirin Mohtashami
Cover design: Denise Maxwell
Author photo: Arash Mohtashami

This book was produced by the collective effort of Women's Press. Women's Press gratefully acknowledges the financial support of the Canada Council and the Ontario Arts Council.

Printed and bound in Canada
1 2 3 4 5   1999 1998 1997 1996 1995

Many thanks to:

Nancy Armstrong, Dr. Rivanne Sandler for her academic consultation, and Ann Decter, co-managing editor at Women's Press.

Also thanks to:

Ontario Arts Council and Canada Arts Council whose financial assistance helped me to spend my time on this book.

Contents

Stories and *Poems*

Introduction

Mehri Yalfani's style of writing is linked to the short story genre favoured by Iranian prose writers of the 1960s-1970s.

The taste for prose literature was slow to develop in a culture which regarded poetry as the quintessential form of literary expression. However, the establishment of a new political system in the 1920s began a series of profound changes in Iranian life. Not the least of these changes was the development of a small, intensely interested audience for radically new forms of literature such as free verse poetry and the short story.

From its beginning, non-traditional Iranian literature of the twentieth century was committed to social and cultural (and even political) reform. The choice of plain language, simple sentence structure, and content devoted to social issues was evidence, not only of a writer's turning away from the ornate literary tradition of the past, but from the social system associated with that tradition. Writers created their own words (the Persian language lends itself to such literary "tricks") to express new and dissenting concepts. Sentences were streamlined. The over-use of adjectives, favoured by writers of the past, was regarded by a new generation of writers as the enemy of serious content.

The short story in particular, provided the stage for life dramas drawn primarily from the underclasses of a newly-emerging economy. The lives of peasants and rural migrants to the city became the focus of literary interest. The elite, the unscrupulous who used their power to further their own interests, the pretensions of the newly-rich were satirized. The writer sought protection from criticism (and worse) in veiled suggestions, in symbolic language. One feature of Yalfani's writing that readers are bound to notice is her use of nature, of images drawn from nature, to provide a clue to the emotional state of characters who do not always fully express their feelings. Women play a role in twentieth-century Iranian literature, more often than not as secondary, weakly-drawn figures. Female characters tend to be utilized as minor players, as symbols of social injustice or icons. In this particular area, the writing of Mehri Yalfani openly parts company with the literary tradition of the past. Her stories pull the reader into the worlds of palpably human women characters who are at the very centre of her literary creation.

Mehri Yalfani creates female characters who are key figures in their own dramas. Events beyond their control have robbed them of happiness, security, a feeling of well-being. Yet Yalfani's characters do their utmost to cope. They face repression at the levels of domestic life and the larger polity. From different social backgrounds, they experience in equal share, cruelty and upheaval, the sadness of leaving the familiar behind. Uncertainty is their constant companion, no matter if the setting is Iran or if many miles separate the characters from their original home.

Yalfani's stories are open-ended, almost as if unfinished, as if awaiting further developments. Women face new situations. They find new ways of supporting themselves. There is no firm resolution of life's sorrows in Yalfani's writing, no epiphany of understanding of, or from, experience. The reader is given a brief glimpse into the lives of Yalfani's characters.

Dr. Rivanne Sandler
Associate Professor,
University of Toronto,
Toronto, Canada
August 1995

8

Homa

Her hands
two branches
flaming to eternity
her feet rooted
deep
in history
in women, in healing women

set on fire.

Set herself
        on fire
flames
spreading
        everywhere
in this big world
burning in a tiny house
on the other side
of the hemisphere.

Sang a song
with her flames
loud — loudly
reaching to the sky
to God
screaming
NO   NO   NO

*for Homa Darabi, a physician who set herself on fire to protest
the obligatory veil in Iran*

~ The Full Moon in the Window ~

It seemed as though someone had awakened Tara,
put his hand on her shoulder and said, "Get up, get up;
something is going to happen. They are coming." As though
someone had stared at her so fiercely she could feel it with
her eyes closed. Her heart started to beat faster. What was
happening? She saw the moon. Or did the moon see her?
Perhaps the moon had stared at her, a full moon that filled
the window. Lying beside Farzad, she could see the moon
in the window.

She had forgotten to pull down the blind before going to
sleep. She tried to remember what time she went to sleep
last night. Eleven? No, later. She had read a little. She had
seen the moon early in the evening, rising from the horizon
like a copper plate. Then, every time she came to the
bedroom the moon was smaller, but brighter. It seemed lost
among the city's lights. And now it was sitting in front of her,
shining brighter than the other stars in the darkness, lighting
the room.

Tara looked at the clock. There wasn't enough light to
see it well. Perhaps the moon's light had blinded her. She
looked carefully, it was two thirty-five. She heard Farzad
breathing. He slept on his side and breathed quietly, like a
bird with his eyes closed. And the baby...

She lifted her head and looked at him. He was asleep

too, with his fist in front of his face, as if he wanted to protect himself from a blow. Tara lay her head down on the pillow and looked at moon, lonely and silent in the deep darkness.

She wished the moon could be full, round and bright forever. Whenever she saw the moon with its darkened edge, she felt sad. She liked the moon. The moon's beauty was unique. More beautiful than the sun, more beautiful than those billions of stars that twinkled with joy. The moon was a lagoon; motionless and silent. But beautiful. Supposedly conquered by Man, it was still an untouched virgin. Lonely and forlorn in the deep darkness. The moon's loneliness made Tara feel sad. If there could be a few moons in the sky, just a few, not millions or billions, the moon wouldn't be lonely any more, and Tara wouldn't feel sad for the moon with its darkened edge.

Tara was dreaming with her eyes open, looking at the moon and watching the moon look at her. As if she was the only person on the earth, and the moon wanted to devote its beauty to her.

Farzad rolled onto his back. Tara turned and looked at him. She wanted to wake him up and show him the moon, spend an hour or so looking at the moon; like other nights, in the country, or seashore, when they sat on the veranda or on the beach at midnight, listening to the silent mountains or the sound of the sea and admiring the full moon. They felt sorry for the moon wandering and turning around the earth forever, without getting light or heat or life from it.

Tara heard footsteps, then the whispering of a few men. Her heart beat in her throat and her ears. She sat up on the bed, put her hand on Farzad's shoulder and woke him up.

"What is it?"

"I heard a noise."

Farzad sat up on the bed too. He ran his hand through

his dishevelled hair. He listened. The baby breathed loudly, as if an 'oh' left in his chest was suddenly released.

"Do you hear?"

"No, I don't hear anything."

"I do. Listen. They are behind the door. They're here. Finally they've come."

Tara put her hand on Farzad's shoulder. Her black hair slipped down her right shoulder and poured on to her chest. Fear shimmered in her black eyes.

"What we are going to do? How do we escape? The baby? What do we do with the baby? Get up and get dressed."

Farzad took her face in his hands. "Wait. Listen. I don't hear a noise. Let's think about it. If they have come, there is no way to escape. How can we escape?"

She got close to him and repeated, "How?"

He listened.

"Don't you hear? They're whispering. They're behind the door. They're unlocking the door. Don't you hear?"

"No, I don't hear anything."

He wanted to get up and look through the keyhole. Tara grasped his elbow. "No, don't go. They'll see you. Perhaps they have a gun. Not perhaps, for sure they have. Perhaps they will kill us right now. Oh my God. My baby! What will happen to my baby? If they kill him first! If they kill you! If..."

Farzad put his hand over her mouth. Struggling to control his anger, he said kindly, "Be quiet, please be quiet."

"Why don't you hear? You have a sensitive ear, why don't you hear?"

"I don't hear. Perhaps I'm still asleep, or not awake enough yet. If you would just be quiet."

They were quiet.

"Tara..."

She was bewildered in the silence. The noises disappeared, no whispering, no key turning in the door lock. "Do you still hear them?"

"No, I think they've gone."

"Don't you think you were dreaming?"

"Dreaming? No, I was awake. I was looking at the moon." And she looked at the window. The moon had gone, lost behind the highrise which faced their room.

"The moon?" And he looked out the window too.

"Where is the moon?"

"Gone."

"Gone below the horizon?"

"No, it is lost."

He put his hand on her shoulder, "It's better to sleep now."

They lay down. Tara put her head on Farzad's shoulder. "Sleep?"

"Yes, sleep. It was just a nightmare, or perhaps you had a bad dream."

"I wasn't dreaming. I was awake. I heard their voices. They will come. I know that they will come. They will take you. Perhaps they will take me too. Then what will happen to the baby?"

"Don't think about that. Don't think about that right now."

"How can I not think? It's not in my control. Do you think that I like to think about it? They are not good dreams. I don't like to think about them, but is it in my control? I always think about it, always."

"But try, try not to think. Just think about now, you and me and the baby are together."

"But just a few minutes ago. Have you forgotten? They came to take you, and perhaps me too. And then...then what would happen to us? Everything would be over. Everything would be destroyed, our home, our serenity, our happiness, our love, our baby, our days and nights, our friends, our family, all. Yes, all. And if they kill you, or me, or the baby, or all three of us..."

Farzad put his hand over her mouth gently. "Put these nightmares out of your mind. Think just about this moment."

"This moment? But this moment is ruined. Look. The moon is gone too. A few minutes ago it was so beautiful, full and bright in front of the window. It was staring through the window into the room. Perhaps it wanted to wake me up. Wanted me to hear them. Didn't want me to be grabbed in my sleep. Imagine, you are having a nice dream when they rush in. I would die of fear. If I heard their steps, my heart would come out of my chest. And if I were to see them close to me, beside my bed... imagine it. What would you do?"

"Me? I have never thought about it."

"Never?"

"No."

"You're lying. I know that you're lying. How is it possible? You know that one day they will come, and when they do, they won't give us a chance. You can't struggle. You have to surrender. They'll handcuff you. Perhaps... Not perhaps, for sure, they will beat you till you fall. They won't have any sympathy for you. No pity at all. Perhaps they'll kill your baby in front of you. Or rape me, your wife, spit in my face, or in your face. Perhaps they will kick your head until you die, or my head. Perhaps they will crush your baby under their feet, perhaps..."

He put his hand over her mouth and said angrily, "Be quiet."

She threw his hand away from her mouth and sat up in

14

the bed. Her soft black hair covered her shoulders. The room was dark. A nightlight cast red above the baby's head. Tara's eyes looked red. "Ha? Tell me. What would you do then?"

"What do you think we should do?"

She put her head on his chest and sobbed. "I'm afraid. I'm afraid. They'll come, I know."

"Tell me what can I do? What can I do so you won't be afraid."

She lifted her head from his chest. Farzad caught her shoulder, pressed her head gently to himself. "You shouldn't think about it. It's not just you."

"But I want to live."

"I want to live too."

"And you're not afraid?"

He said nothing. He was afraid too. Fear was with him like breathing. But he didn't talk about it.

"No."

"No?"

"No."

"How can that be? Tell me why you aren't afraid. You're not afraid of death, of torture? Of them murdering your baby in front of you, and your wife..."

He put his hands over her mouth again. "Please, that's enough."

Tara cried, "Tell me why you're not afraid. Tell me why."

"I'm afraid too. Of course. I'm always afraid."

She put her head on his shoulder and sobbed.

"We are all afraid. But, what will happen to the baby then? He will grow up in fear."

She took her head from Farzad's shoulder and looked into his eyes. "Will he grow up? Will he grow up in fear?"

"Until the time..."

"Yes, until then. It's a long time to live in fear, to sleep

15

in fear, to wake up in fear, to eat in fear, and to look at the full moon in the window in fear."

"Hush."

Tara turned and looked at him.

"What is it?"

"Do you hear?"

"What?"

"The noise. The whispering noise."

Tara listened. She stared at the door and the darkness behind it and listened.

"No, I don't hear anything."

"But I do. The sound of a key. They're turning the key and unlocking the door."

"You're imagining it, there is no noise."

"I'm not imagining it. I hear it. Listen."

Tara listened quietly.

~ Someone at the Door ~

It was one of those days when I felt happy for no reason, yet I had a strange suspicion that something might be about happen to my family. I'm not superstitious, but many times, just as I was feeling really happy, something bad would happen. There was no reason for my joy, but I was excited. Those were the days when horror and fear wandered everywhere like living creatures; yet I was happy — perhaps simply because my children were at home, my husband at work, and no danger threatened us.

I had been sitting on the veranda that evening. Nastran was in her room, reading. Arash and Siavoush were playing Iran-Iraq war with toy soldiers. I heard the imitated noise of machine guns. Ignoring them, my mind drifted, enjoying the peaceful silence.

As I gazed at the Plane tree where sparrows were chirping happily among the branches, I heard a short ring. First I thought I'd imagined it. But I moved to the courtyard door, and I heard it again. I opened the door quickly. There was a girl, about sixteen or seventeen, in a black veil from head to toe, fear in her eyes, lips trembling. She said, "They're following me. May I come in for a few minutes? I'll leave as soon as they go away."

It was as if I'd seen a leper. I slammed the door and rushed into the yard. My heart began to beat quickly. I thought I might faint. I waited for the door bell again, but there was silence. I couldn't even hear footsteps. I went into the kitchen where I could see the street without being noticed. My heart was still racing, my feet like ice. Fortunately, none of the children had heard the door bell.

I stood by the window for a while. There was no one in the street. A white Paykan drove into the street and I could see two bearded *pasdars*, uniformed security police in the back seat. I was horrified, expecting the car to stop and them to get out and ring our door bell. The car drove on. My heart calmed a bit, but the image of the girl — black eyes, small nose, and trembling lips — stayed with me. I hated her. She had no right to ring my door bell, to disturb my happiness. I tried to convince myself I was right to send her away. If the *pasdars* were to find her in my home, what would become of us? It would be all over. But, in fact, they didn't ring our door bell. They drove past without a glance. If I had given the girl shelter, she would be safe. A thorn lodged in my heart, and the sweat of shame beaded on my forehead. I felt as if I had committed a terrible sin. My heart ached with regret for what I'd done. Someone seemed to be telling me, "Go and get the girl." Then, the same Paykan approached again, with two men in the back seat, bearded like the driver who was also in uniform. A black-veiled woman sat between them. I couldn't see her face. She was just a black shape between the men.

I felt faint. There was a lump in my throat. I was almost in tears when Nastran came in and headed to the refrigerator for something to eat. She ignored me as usual, passing by like a shadow. I went to my bedroom which looked onto the main street and saw the Paykan again at the intersection. I was right, a veiled woman was sitting between the guards. I wished I could see her face.

As I sat on the edge of my bed, I looked at myself in the dressing table mirror and felt disgusted. My happiness soured to contempt and humiliation. I recalled stories of political prisoners being tortured. I imagined this happening to the girl. My life had shattered when I drove her away, a moment when I didn't recognize myself. When my real self, mean and cruel, emerged from behind a mask of generosity. Fear that lived in me like a monster overcame me, tossing away my values like so much scrap paper. I buried my face in my hand. I didn't know myself anymore. Yet someone whispered in my ear, "You were right to send her away. You're not responsible for her life, only for your own family. If you had given her refuge, they would certainly have found her. And you don't know her ideology or to what political party she belonged. How do you know that she's really innocent?"

None of these justifications prevented my guilty feelings. I was sure the girl had been arrested and taken to jail. I knew about the terrible tortures prisoners endured; rape before execution... I saw her frightened black eyes, trembling lips and smooth skin, as pale as if the blood had been drained from her body. I imagined Nastran in her place and felt an unbidden scream gather in my throat. I forced myself to be quiet.

When Nader came home, he found me upset in the bedroom. "What happened?" he asked.

I started crying hysterically, unable to say a word.

The doctor visited me. He couldn't make me talk either. All the time I saw the girl's innocent face, her naked body tortured, raped by many guards. Her cries filled my ears. I wanted to scream out too.

I fell asleep with a sedative. When I awoke, it seemed to be from a nightmare. Trying not to think about the girl, I felt I had become another person. Nader and the children were around me, looking at me as if I had changed. I felt weighed down, abandoned on a deserted island. When I started to cry again, Nader was astonished. Nobody knew what was going on inside me. When I saw Nastran go to the telephone to call the doctor, I said, "It's not necessary to call the doctor, I feel okay."

I tried to hold back the tears and endure my suffering, humiliation and remorse. But it wasn't easy. It drove me mad. I had to convince myself to accept that I had no choice but to drive the girl away. But the hideousness of my action seemed so enormous I didn't dare talk about it with Nader or the children. I don't remember how long I spent like that. Crying hysterically, screaming, then falling asleep with a tranquilliser.

Now with enormous effort, I lead a normal life. I work, I cook, I take care of my family, and I do the housework. Day and night pass for me as they pass for others. I'm haunted by the vision of someone, waiting behind the door for me to open it — a sixteen or seventeen year old girl, black veil covering her body, fearful black eyes, lips trembling. I get up to open the door for her, then I remember the girl sitting between the two guards, being taken to jail in the white Paykan. Every day I read all the names of women who are executed in the daily paper. I don't know whether her name is among them or not.

Pasdar — revolutionary guard
Paykan — car manufactured in Iran

Sentenced to Stoning

Your body for sale
your body in soil
your reward for love
stoning
            to death.

Your body planted
            in soil
innocent hands throwing
            stones.

You sprout
in virtuous hearts
your hands
            branches
your feet
            roots
you grow.

Your memories
dance in empty
                        houses
sinful lovers burning
                        their fingers.

You sprout
in virtuous hearts.

~ Parastoo ~

"You see, she has become a swallow," my sister said.

"What do you mean?" I said. "Is it possible for a human being to become a bird?"

"It's happened. Parastoo did what she wanted."

I didn't believe it. I was sure she had run away. "Are you sure she didn't run away?"

She looked at me crossly.

Haji, my sister's husband, said, "Whether she's flown up to the sky or swooped down to the ground, I will find her and kill her. The biggest piece left of her will be her ear. She is shameless, she shows no respect for her father."

"There she is in the cage," my sister said. "Why are you making God angry? Where would she have gone? When? She slept beside me all last night. It was dawn when I found she was not in bed."

The bird in her cage stared at us in silence. Was it really Parastoo? How innocent she looked! What was she thinking about? Parastoo was like this too, always silent, and she seemed to be speaking with her eyes.

Yesterday, I asked her, "Why are you so depressed?"

"Auntie, you know," she said. "I don't want to do it."

"There is no use fighting it," I said. "You get nowhere by getting upset. It's better to go along with it."

"I don't love him. How can I marry him?"

"Friendship and love come later."

Parastoo said nothing. Just looked at me. She certainly had a plan in mind. But how did she become a bird?

Haji said, "She's become a devil, she should be killed."

He had gone to the Mosque and got permission from the Mullah to kill her. The bird was in her cage, staring at us as we talked about Haji's intention to kill her.

"Haji, how can you kill an innocent bird?" I said.

Haji was talking about killing the bird and I was arguing that Parastoo was not the bird in the cage when my sister fainted. She came round with a glass of water and a temple massage. I said, "Let her go. The bird should be free to follow her mate."

"She is not a bird," Haji said. "She is the devil. She should be killed." He took the cage to the backyard. Hamid and Vahid just stood there and didn't dare say a word to their father. My sister and I followed, to rescue the bird.

"Haji," I said. "Just imagine that it's Parastoo and God wishes to punish her by transforming her into a bird. Why do you stain your hands with your daughter's blood? How will you answer to God?"

"It's better for you not to interfere. I've got a *fatwa* for her death. If she remains alive, there will be more sins. Is it not enough that she has shamed me in front of our relatives? What should I do with her? Take care of her in my house and feed her? By tomorrow she'll have something else up her sleeve."

"Haji, it's better to be rational," I pleaded. "Who believes that a human being can become a bird? This is not Parastoo. Parastoo has fled."

He stared at me crossly. I thought he wanted to kill me.

"You know where she is. Tell me where she has gone, otherwise I'll kill you too."

"What are you doing wise guy?" my sister interrupted. "Does she know anything about her? Parastoo was with me last night. You were there too. Didn't you see her early this morning? Have you lost your head? Early this morning didn't you see the black bird flying about the room, trying to escape! Didn't you say yourself that it's Parastoo! How can you change your mind? Why are you making trouble for yourself? Why are you putting words in people's mouths?"

She turned to me, "I didn't expect you to say such things. Where is a fifteen-year-old girl going to go?"

"I feel sorry for the bird. It's a big sin to kill her. It's better to let her go free," I said.

Haji took the bird out of the cage, ignoring our pleas. The bird screeched and tried to get free. But Haji had the knife between his teeth and grabbed the bird with both hands. He put its head in the pool for a drink. But the bird didn't want to. Haji laid it down, the knife still between his teeth, spread its wings and stood on each of them. He sharpened the knife on the stone edge of the pool.

We were all paralysed watching Haji. Even Hamid and Vahid didn't dare approach their father. Haji pressed the blade to the bird's throat. She screeched loudly, twisted and escaped. She flew away. She might not be able to get past the wall of the yard. Haji followed. She flapped and flew higher, cleared the wall and disappeared into the vast sky.

Six months passed. I told my sister, "Forget it. It's finished."

But she didn't forget. She blamed herself. Six months had

passed, but she had not forgotten. She said, "I saw Parastoo in the street yesterday."

"It was a dream."

"No, it was not a dream. Are you saying that I don't know my own child!"

"If you saw her why didn't you talk to her? Why didn't you ask her to come back home?"

"When I got close to her," she said, "she flapped her wings and flew away."

My sister died. Her memorial ceremony was yesterday. Parastoo came back. She was herself. She hasn't changed at all since last year. She came in quietly and sat beside the door. She hid her face behind the black *chador* and cried. Nobody recognized her, except me. I didn't take my eyes off her. I wanted to sit beside her and ask her why she fled from home and left a swallow in her place? But Parastoo didn't show her face. While I was saying goodbye to a second cousin, I saw her leave the room. I followed her, rushing down the stairs. She wasn't in the yard. A black bird was sitting on the plane tree gazing at the room where the Koran was being read. My heart pounded. Was it Parastoo?

Parastoo — Farsi: girl's name meaning swallow
fatwa — a Mullah's ruling

The First Day Without Home

No sun
        no rain
shadow of clouds
sound of vagueness.

A hazy room — an empty room
cockroaches — everywhere
is this all I deserve?

I narrated my life
my whole life
filed on
                a paper.

Date of birth
date of marriage
date of immigration
date of happy days
                sad days
date of not being a
                human being
date of being
                nothing.

My whole life
        in a file.
getting pale — old
boring to read.

I am here without
          home
a home
that never belonged to me
a home
I made it
        clean
a home
I made it
a home
a home
that never was
          mine.

Am I going to be born
            again
on this day
      or…

In An Unknown House

In an unknown house
with people — with faces
and sounds far from
                    me.

In a land
with a strange language
I am sharing
                    myself
with vagueness — with window
and snow — coming down
                    sadly.

A voice in the air
a wondering voice
talking about a
                    man
never offering his hand to
                    anyone.

It's snowing
I'm sharing my heart
with windows —bare trees
sadly snowing.

I'm sharing my stories — my memories
and all my past
left in so many houses
with nothing.

I have an odd time
with my hands
with my eyes
hunting for a friendly
            look.

Too many people — here
all sad — all ghostly
walking around
and looking for
                someone
banished in hate.

I should discover myself
                again.
I should buy a
            bed
and sleep on it alone by
            myself.

Red Leaves

Love me, love me,
                love me
love me and don't ask,
"Why are the leaves of trees green
                        not red?"

Love me
and let me get warm to grow.
I'm planted here
under the ground
frozen to death.

But love me and let me
get warm, grow
be watered by my
                blood
to be a tree
with red leaves not
                green.

You'll find me
in the trees
not in your
                dreams
and I'll see you
as you are.

Love me
just love me
let me get warm to grow
to be a tree
with red leaves
       not green.

For Maral

*"Why are the leaves of trees green not red?" is from a poem
by Maral*

31

LIFE

LIFE, is simple
singing for BIRTH
crying in DEATH.

BUT...
don't cry for me
DEATH is a twin for BIRTH.

Sing for me
with your hands
with your eyes
with your bones
with your heart
beating in joy for life.

Sing for me
with trees — with birds
with no conception of DEATH.

for Nancy and Joe

~ The Other Side of the Border ~

Desert or mountain, which one should we choose?
It wasn't easy to make a decision. We talked about it for
hours and hours. Sometimes we chose the desert, sometimes
the mountains.

Crossing the desert and walking on flat land was perhaps
the easier way. But there was the risk we would be walking
for weeks without finding any shelter or any protection.
There would be days in the sunshine and nights under the
vast, cold sky. There was the risk of being watched. Some
said the desert is not safe at all. They talked about people
who had chosen the desert and never reached their
destination. Perhaps lost in a sandstorm. Others believed if
you are trapped in a sandstorm you can come back, instead
of going forward and getting lost. In fact, walking wasn't
difficult and it was possible to cross the border in a day. But
there was also the risk of wandering in the desert for weeks
or even months. Unlike the mountains, there was no
possibility of hiding behind rocks, or finding shelter from
rain, wind and the guards. Or feeding on wild grasses. The
desert was barren, except for mirages, which gave empty
hope.

For me, climbing the mountains was also not easy. I was
against it because I suffered from vertigo. There was the risk
of becoming lost, the dangers of snow, avalanche, lightning,

wild animals, so many unpredictable things. But I was afraid of deserts too, because of snakes. I had read about deserts and all the poisonous snakes. Even thinking about it made the blood run cold in my body.

"There are snakes in the mountain too," my husband said. "There are scorpions as well. Deserts and mountains are not like a house that can be protected. If you are afraid of cockroaches, how can you face all these dangerous animals?"

"Do we have any other choice?" I said. "What do we do with these two children?"

One day we had got up in the morning, listened to the news on the radio and heard that boys fourteen and older were prohibited from leaving the country. At that time Shahin was fourteen years and eight months, and Afshin thirteen years and nine months. But they were both so tiny that they looked like ten and eleven year olds.

Before that time, we never thought about leaving the country. We hoped that by the time Afshin and Shahin reached the age of military service, the war would be over. Although it was usual to hear in the media that the war would last for 20 years, we didn't believe it. We believed that the war would be over soon. When I learned about the prohibition of children leaving the country, I felt a fire in my body.

With the drills at school and the advertisements for the war in the media, the children were interested in drilling, learning how to use G3 machine guns, Kalashnikov rifles and how to throw grenades. As far back as I could remember, their childish games were always war and James Bond. Shelves in their room were full of plastic soldiers: medieval warriors, Nazi, Vietnamese and American soldiers. Every day they played war in their room, threw grenades and missiles at each other's toys. There was nothing on TV except movies and plays about the war. Posters supporting the war were everywhere. In any family gathering, the most important topic of discussion was the war. The war entered my dreams. And when the bombing started, we waited for a bomb to drop on our heads. We waited to drink the *sherbat shahadat.*

I said to my husband: "Death only occurs once. If we are going to be buried under missiles or bombs or die of fright, then let's take a risk and save ourselves. Perhaps we can find a better world, a world without war, missiles, bombs, and the nightmare of heaven or hell. A world in which we can breathe freely." And I read from Sadie's poems, "Oh Sadie, the sages have said it's honourable to love your homeland, but I can't dishonour myself for the sake of dying here."

We're neither the top of the onion nor the bottom. And as my grandfather used to say, if people allow themselves to become donkeys, then we'll ride them. Danger was on our doorstep. There was no way to avoid it.

We talked about leaving the country for weeks. There was no way to stay. Even if we ignored the fear of being killed and military service for our children, we spent most of our life searching for necessities, standing in long lines for rationed groceries and detergent. Life was nothing but the struggle to survive. We didn't read or watch a movie. I told my husband that if we do nothing and just wait, they will not only take our children from us, but they will turn us into people without feelings or willpower. We would spend all our days and nights thinking about how to find bread, butter, cheese and meat.

So we began to sell our house and our property. We jeopardized our lives to leave the country. It was not easy. We had to ignore seventeen years of memories. Selling the house and furniture seemed like setting them on fire. People didn't value our things the way we did. They wanted to bargain but we had to be quiet and say nothing. We didn't have any other choice; we had to accept it. Things were worth nothing in comparison to the lives of our children. We had to make our decision and leave the country. We were sure that our decision was correct. We hadn't yet decided which way to cross the border. Sometimes we thought about the desert and its advantages, and other times about the mountains.

My husband and my children made me afraid of the mountains. They said climbing wasn't easy for me. I wanted to choose the desert but I insisted on the mountains, just because I didn't want to show my fear. I said, "I'm ready to climb any mountain."

At the last minute we drew lots, and against my inner desire, it was the mountain. We prepared for the departure, and without saying goodbye to our friends or relatives we set out for the border.

We reached the border without any problem, though horror and fear didn't leave us alone. Every minute passed like a year. Time stuck to the trees and village houses on our way. The day we left our homeland behind and reached the border was a long, sad day. We didn't talk to each other at all. We didn't want to talk and disturb each other's thoughts. Fear and anxiety quieted us. Everybody was afraid of transferring their fear to the others. But our reason for this dangerous departure was our future. We knew that beyond these dangerous moments, and across the border, a lovely and enjoyable life was waiting for us. The future was ahead, a sunny, warm day, full of enjoyment.

Finally, we reached the border. It was almost sunset. A high mountain was in front of us. We couldn't see the sun, but it was clear that it had not set yet. We could see golden rays on the top of the mountain. The valleys were in the shadow of sunset and the deep silence made the four of us quiet, saying nothing. We just thought about how to climb the high mountain. We had no choice, it was the way we had chosen. I wanted to say that it was better to choose the desert, but it was useless. With great effort we started to climb, higher with every step. Our thoughts about the future lit our way and pushed us to go higher and higher.

It was no longer night when we reached the first summit. We watched the sun rise like a golden bowl, up out of the horizon to cover the world with its bright light. I remembered a poem from Ferdowsie, "As the bright sun drew its bow/ The gloomy night disappeared out of fear."

It was a good omen, reaching the summit at the same time as the sunrise. I shouted for joy. The four of us danced and sang happily. We sat on the highest rock; our hearts full of joy, love and the glory of conquest. Our homeland behind us was in shadow. It seemed that the sun had never shone on it. But what could we do? Leaving was the only choice. In front of us were mountains and valleys in light. We came down the mountain, but before we reached the valley, another mountain rose in front of us. We looked at each other, surprised. Where did this mountain come from? Was it there all the time and we hadn't noticed it?

Mountains don't just rise up in one night. Again it was sunset and dim shadows made us sad and quiet. But we didn't have time to be disappointed. We had to be determined and climb this mountain too.

Now, so many years have passed, and there is no end to this chain of mountains. My sons are older, with beards and moustaches. White snow covers my husband's hair, and when he climbs a mountain, he feels short of breath. I am old and tired too. I don't know whether there will be another mountain, or if we will find peace and rest. But I know my husband, my sons and I are determined to cross these high, endless mountains. We don't care how high they are. Every day we climb to the summit and sit on the highest rock, to watch the sun rise.

Sherbat shahadat — "the drink of martyrdom." It is a religious belief that a person who was killed in war would automatically go to heaven.

~ Which Elaheh? ~

When I woke him, Ramin started to cry. First I thought, he's sick, with his red cheeks and hoarse voice. I touched his forehead, it wasn't very hot. He didn't want to get out of bed.

He asked, "Do I have to go to school?"

I said, "Yes, it's late. You should hurry up."

"I don't want to go, I have a headache."

I felt his forehead again — it was still a bit hot. He started to cry. Worried, I asked, "What is the matter? Are you in pain?"

"No."

"So, get up, it's getting late."

"I'm not going to school, I don't want to go."

"What nonsense! How can you stay away from school? You have a trip today, have you forgotten?"

"I don't want to go on the trip either, I have a headache."

"Don't be silly. What about me? I have to go to work. If I don't they'll fire me."

"But I don't want to go to school."

I hugged him and lifted him up, but he lay down again, with his back to me. I was getting angry. He was eight years old, but he was behaving like a small child.

"Ramin, don't be a bother," I cried. "I'm going to make

your sandwiches. When I come back, you should be dressed and ready." And I left.

I made the sandwiches and returned to his bedroom, but he was still lying down, face to the wall and motionless. "What's the matter with you?" I said. "It's eight o'clock. When are you going to have your breakfast and leave? Damn it. I have to be at work by nine."

He said nothing. I sat by his bed and tried to be calm, but in fact I was very angry. "Does it hurt?" I asked. "Why don't you say something? You're not a child any more. If you're sick, tell me, I'll take you to a doctor."

He said nothing, blew his nose and moved his hand to his eyes. I saw he was crying. As he turned his head to me, I bent and kissed him. I asked him, "Why are you crying? Don't you like school? Did something happen?"

He said nothing. And now he was crying very loudly. "Tell me what happened. Did you have a dream? Did you have a bad dream?"

He said, "I saw Elaheh in my dream."

I lifted him up. "Okay, let's go into the dining room and have breakfast, and you tell me what you dreamed."

"But I'm not going to school."

"Why?"

"I don't feel like it."

I wanted to laugh, but I didn't. An eight-year-old child is not in the mood? I smiled and said, "You're not in the mood! Me either, I'm not in the mood to go to work. Your father is not in the mood to go to work either. Then where will we get money to pay for food, clothes, or for the rent? Let's not talk about being in the mood. Whether you are in the mood or not you must go to school."

I hugged him, brought him into the dining room and sat

him down on a chair. I put his cereal and milk in front of
him. "Well, tell me about your dream."

He ignored his cereal and me and lowered his head, tears
rolling down his cheeks. I guessed he had dreamed about
Elaheh, Nahid's daughter. We don't see each other often.
Nahid is studying at university and is always busy.

I said, "Do you miss her? I'll call this weekend and if she
is not busy, we'll go and see her." Elaheh is good with
children.

"I didn't dream of that Elaheh."

"So, which one?"

"I don't know. I've forgotten her mother's name."

"Is she our friend from here?"

"No."

"In Iran?"

"No."

"In Turkey?"

"No."

"In Germany?"

"No."

"In Bulgaria?"

He was surprised, "Bulgaria? Where's Bulgaria?"

"Don't you remember when we were travelling from
Turkey to Germany, they detained us in Bulgaria? Don't you
remember Mrs. Sarmadi's daughter? She was eight years old
— older than you. Her name was Elaheh."

He thought a little, "Did she wear a blue and white dress?"

What a question! How could I remember the girl's dress.
I just remember that she had pretty dresses, and brown hair,
honey coloured eyes. Her mother always combed her hair in
two pigtails and tied them in coloured ribbons. I was sure
Ramin had been dreaming about her. That few days that we
travelled together, Ramin was friendly with her. Ramin was

six years old and the girl was eight. She was a bossy girl, and Ramin obeyed her.

"I'm sure you're talking about that girl," I said.

"Did she wear a white and blue dress?"

"I don't remember because she changed her dress every day. But she had brown hair, and her eyes were like honey."

"Honey? What do you mean?" he asked with surprise.

I realized he didn't understand me. "It's a light colour, not like your eyes which are black."

"I don't remember what colour my Elaheh's eyes were, but she had on a blue dress, and her collar was made of white lace. We were playing together, like when we were children."

"Oh," I said. "I remember, you're talking about your Aunt Farzaneh, and Elaheh, her daughter."

"Which Aunt Farzaneh?" He was surprised.

"Your real aunt, my sister, in Iran."

I brought our photo album and showed him a picture of Farzaneh, with her husband and Elaheh. He looked at it. "No, it's not her, she's a baby."

I was exhausted. The clock showed ten minutes past eight. He hadn't had his breakfast and hadn't dressed.

"Sweetie, have your breakfast, it's getting late."

He got up from the chair and sat on the sofa, embraced his knees and said, "I'm not going to school to day. I miss Elaheh."

Tears streamed down his face.

I lost my patience and shouted at him, "Why are you behaving like a baby? How do I know which Elaheh you're talking about? Which country does she come from?"

As the tears flowed down his face he asked, "Does every country have an Elaheh?"

"The countries we've lived in and passed through, each one of them had an Elaheh who you liked."

"Then who was the one who wore the blue dress?"

I got really angry and shouted, "The Elaheh in the cemetery."

"You mean my Elaheh is dead?" he cried loudly. "The one who was my friend? We had promised to get married when we grew older."

I smiled to myself and thought, what a surprise. Such a small child can fall in love and make plans to marry! Then I said, "Oh really, congratulations! So you were in love, and I didn't know."

His eyes still brimming with tears, he laughed and said, "Did I do something bad?"

"No. Love is not bad."

Ramin's tears stopped, his face covered with a childish grin. "Yes it's good." And then again he asked me, "Tell me what happened to her? Where is she?" And he put the problem in my lap again, without offering any clue to solve it.

"I'll have to think about that," I said. "It's not easy for me to find the Elaheh of your dreams. First of all eat breakfast quickly, get dressed, and get going to school, I have to go to work. Then when school is finished and work is finished, we can think about it. Maybe we'll remember where she is — the Elaheh of your dreams."

He accepted my logic and sat down at the table. We got ready as fast as we could.

I sent him to school with his lunch box in his hand. As I lost him in the crowd of children, I wondered, "In which country did the child lose his first love?"

Elaheh — female name meaning goddess

~ Dead End Alleys ~

When we reached the end of the alley in that old neighbourhood, with its clay walls and small windows, I said, "It is a dead end."

"There must be an exit," Golnar answered.

There wasn't one. It was a narrow, covered alley. We kept on going, but there wasn't any exit. She said, "Let's explore."

I didn't want to and turned back. How long could we wander in these deserted, empty alleys? But it was hard to stay at home too. The afternoons were so long. In the summertimes it was worse. If Baba was at home, it was hard to breathe. He would kill me with the contempt in his eyes. Golnar said, "You're not the only one."

This morning when she called, her voice was different. She was happy. I could tell. We had been friends since the first year of high school. We wrote the university entrance exams several times, I don't remember how many. We passed the exams with the same results. Golnar said, "I don't know how to study."

I didn't know either. We went to the preparation course too, it didn't work. This year I didn't try. Maman said, "Anyhow, there might be a chance." No, there was not. I had no hope. Golnar used to say, "What we learned is all wet." I like her. She takes things easy, and makes fun of everything. When I am with her, my worries fade. This morning when she called, she was happy. What had happened? Perhaps she had bought some new fabric and wanted to come to our house, or she wanted me to go to hers. Maman doesn't let me go out. I have to get her permission and I'm not in the mood to do that. I stayed in my room and closed the door.

"Are you waiting for your chickens to hatch?" Kamran teased.

I wasn't in the mood. Maman talked about other girls. Baba didn't look at me at all. I knew what his eyes said: old maid.

Obstinately, I stayed in my room. Maman shouted at me, but I didn't answer. She stood by my door and spoke to me angrily, "What is the problem? Are you in mourning? Go and wash the dishes."

"Good news!" Golnar had said.

What was her good news so early in the morning? "Are you listening?" she said.

"Yes," I answered.

"I'm going to get married. Can you imagine that?"

I was astounded. Was she dreaming? Just yesterday we reached that dead-end alley in that deserted neighbourhood and I said, "How do you find them?"

"They're there."

She went the wrong way deliberately. She likes adventure. "What can be bad? Let's go and find out where it ends."

"Why do you choose a way you don't know?" I said.

"I want to learn," she had answered.

"Are you asleep? I'm going to get married."

"When? Did you meet him after midnight?"

"No, a few days ago. But it doesn't matter. Shahin says he is perfect. Reza is from America and he will be going back. He will take me to America. No, we will marry here, and he will leave first, and later on I'll follow him."

"Have you seen him before?"

"Yes, I saw him when he came to our home with Shahin. He is wonderful. You know, I couldn't have dreamed him up. I'm lucky he didn't see you first, otherwise he would have fallen in love with you."

"Does he love you?"

"I think so."

"It's a miracle."

Maman asked who was on the phone so early in the morning. I didn't answer her. I felt depressed. If Golnar left, who would I go wandering with? Summer afternoons were so long. It was not good to be seen in the main streets every day. It made us stand out in this small town. Answering Baba's questions tried my patience. Golnar knows so many interesting routes. She's lucky. She doesn't worry about things. She says, "What can I do? I can't go into the street and shout, "Hey men, I have to marry.' Damn all of them. I don't care."

And now she was very happy. It was clear from her voice. She said, "I'll tell you everything." But then quickly broke off. Maman sighed and said, "One just needs a little luck."

I didn't have luck. I was prettier than Golnar. She used to say, "I bet that you will marry before me." But she lost that bet.

She phoned many times a day! Maman answered the phone and said, "It's for you." Golnar spoke again about Reza, as if she had known him for years, and told me many things about him.

"Did you know him before? " I asked.

"He has been at our house a couple of times," she said. "He is Shahin's friend. Shahin told me he's attractive."

I went to my room and closed the door. Maman said, "Do something with yourself, like Golnar." Now Golnar is in her good book. Until yesterday I couldn't mention her name. "That rude, old maid!" Maman would say. "Leave her. Don't go walking with her. People talk behind your back."

Golnar came to our home. Maman greeted her warmly. She didn't let her come to my room — took her to the living room. She wished her a happy marriage, and looked at her as though there was a star on her forehead. I had gone to make some sherbat for Golnar. Maman came to the kitchen and said, "Bring some fruit too." When she looked at me I saw the disappointment in her eyes. She sighed and said, "Just a little luck."

Yes I know, I'm not lucky. What can I do? I can't get a man to descend from heaven just for me. It's not something you can buy easily. As Golnar used to say, "Damn them all. I don't care about them."

Golnar talked a lot about Reza. The phone rang. It was Reza asking for her. She ran out as if she was on fire. She disappeared, forgetting to say goodbye.

The day of her marriage Golnar was very happy, floating on air. She said to me, "Smile. Your turn will come soon."

"My turn!" I don't need it. I hate everyone. Men, women, Maman, Kamran with his sarcasm. Baba with his indifference and contemptuous look. I don't need anybody. I locked myself in my room.

Maman said, "Don't you want to go to the marriage ceremony?" No, I didn't. Maman was ready. Baba and Kamran too. Baba wore a red tie. I wanted to ask, "Why red?" I didn't. I was not in the mood. Maman had a lot of make-up on. She said, "You too, try some make-up. Try some lipstick." I didn't. There won't be another Reza to make-up for. I was not in the mood for this sort of thing. I hated everything.

Kamran had said, "You should try the university exam. Maybe you have a chance."

No, I didn't. With all the recent graduates there was no place for me. He also tried for six years but he didn't succeed. He works with Baba. Baba bought the store because of him. He was retired. I asked to work in the store too. "I like working as a salesperson."

He looked at me crossly, "There is no place for women in the store."

"How could you work with men? Don't even consider it. They won't let you work," Golnar said when I told her. I dropped it. In the afternoons we wandered in the alleys. When we came to a dead end, Golnar said, "There should be an exit. There's no harm trying."

I was afraid. "We may get lost."

"If you're afraid, there's more chance of getting lost," Golnar said.

When we got to the wedding, Golnar said, "Why so late! You are my oldest friend."

Maman whispered, "She is already across the bridge." But I'm still here. Damn them. I'm tired. Everyone looked at me. I read "Old Maid" in their eyes.

Maman had said, "Wear your white dress. You look younger in that dress."

I wanted to ask, "How much younger? Less than twenty-six?" But I said nothing. I wasn't in the mood. I didn't like looking at anybody. They're all the same, "Old Maid" written in their eyes.

"Let me go to Tehran and find a job." Baba looked at me angrily and said nothing.

Maman said, "Don't talk about it any more, he gets angry."

I was silent. I've run out of patience with them.

Golnar doesn't call any more. She is happy with Reza. I haven't heard from her for three days. Maman said, "You call her." I didn't.

The phone rang. "Come, it's Golnar." Maman said. Golnar laughed loudly and said, "Do you have time? We want to come over. We have good news."

"What is it? Tell me," I said.

"When I come over I will," she said.

She told me when we were in the kitchen. My heart stopped for a few seconds. "Are you ready to come to America?" she asked.

"Me?"

"Yes, you."

"How?"

"Reza likes you and he wants you to marry his friend who lives in America. Sohrab can't come to Iran because of military service, but he would like to marry an Iranian girl. A brand new one, do you understand what I mean?"

"Me?"

"Yes, you. Why are you fainting?"

I couldn't believe it. Was it be possible? Me! America! Golnar said in my ear, "Saviour."

And I said involuntarily, "The Saviour sleeps in the grave."

Baba no longer frowns at me. Now that I have a marriage contract, he says I can come and work in the store. I didn't accept. I'm studying English. Sohrab has sent me a letter and money. He said that studying in university is not difficult. You just have to pass the English exam. Kamran is envious of me.

Maman lifted the receiver and seemed to get an electric shock. "Come here, it's Sohrab, from America."

I couldn't speak.

He said, "Are you ready to marry me?"

"With great pleasure," I said.

Maman said, "How polite you were."

Reza showed me Sohrab's photo, a photo of his face, and said, "He is not so handsome."

Maman said, "It doesn't matter. It's not like he's a woman."

How tired he looked.

Kamran asked, "Is he ill?"

Reza said, "No, he works. He works hard. He has a business."

Baba asked, "What does that mean?"

"It means he has a store," Reza explained.

"Doesn't he study?"

"He does. He works and studies. He is quite wealthy."

Sohrab sent me money. He sent me money twice. I went to the English course. I learned the sentences by heart.

Golnar said, "Don't read too much, you'll mix them up."

I'm going to America to be with Golnar. We abandoned the dead-end alleys and went to the English course, Golnar and I, laughing. Golnar left two months ahead of me. "I will come to the airport. Don't be afraid," she said.

I wasn't afraid. I had the marriage contract.

"When I see Sohrab, I'll write you about him," she said.

"It seems he works hard," Kamran said. "He looks tired. Be careful that he's not sick."

"No, he is not," Reza said.

"If only he could be like Reza," Maman said.

Was I afraid? I didn't know. When I thought about Sohrab, all the dead-end alleys led to a garden in full bloom, to Golnar saying "How do we know, maybe this alley leads to paradise." Golnar liked to make fun of everything. She laughed at everything. When she left, I felt very sad. "Take it easy," she said. "Your turn will come soon. Flying over the ocean."

"You have left dead-end alleys behind."

"Yes I have to move on, to experience life. I shouldn't be afraid. Don't you be afraid either."

I wasn't afraid. When I thought about Sohrab, I felt happy. There was someone across the ocean who was thinking about me. He wrote to me, he sent me money. There was someone across the ocean who connected dead-end alleys to gardens. Baba didn't ignore me any more. Kamran wasn't sarcastic with me any more. Maman was nice to me. There was someone across the ocean whose ring I wore and who was taking me out of my room. In the English course everybody looked at me jealously.

The day I left, Maman talked about this and that. Baba wrote a letter for my unseen groom, and called me, "Mail order bride." When he read the letter, we all laughed. "I am not a mail order parcel," I said. I wanted to ask him to change the letter, but I didn't. I was afraid he would be angry with me.

"Don't be afraid," Golnar said. "Say what you want to say. The sky won't fall in. Don't be afraid of a dead-end alley either, keep going. If they have no exit, you can turn back."

Maman says, "Words once spoken are like poured oil, it's not possible to collect them again."

I said nothing. Let him think that I'm a mail order parcel. I don't care. I think of a man, waiting for me across the ocean.

I sat in the airplane and thought about what lay across the ocean. My sadness was gone, left behind in my room with the small window that didn't let in enough light, even in daytime. I was so happy. I looked at the water below; freedom and love waited for me.

At the airport, I recognized Golnar first, then Reza; they were holding hands. People looked strange to me. Such odd features they had! What language were they speaking? A large Black man came toward me and said something. I didn't understand him. I saw Golnar. How happy she was. Reza had his hand around her waist. A man stand behind them. Who was he? Why was Sohrab not there?

What had the Black man said? Golnar laughed loudly and said, "Don't be afraid, their accent is different. I felt the same way."

She took hold of my hand and put it in the hand of the man who was standing back. He seemed afraid to come closer. He had a smile on his face. Who was he?

"Sohrab," Golnar said. "Come closer, here is your wife."

Who was his wife?

"Kiss your wife," Golnar said. Laughing again, she leaned over to Reza. Reza looked at me.

I was confused. I touched the man's cold hand and shivered. He looked so tired!

"Be careful," Kamran had said. "He looks sick. Is he an addict?"

All around me people spoke a strange language. The words on the signboards along the wall were unfamiliar too. I pulled my hand out of his hand and looked behind me, remembering dead-end alleyways. Was there a way back?

"The Saviour sleeps in the grave" is from a poem by the well-known Iranian poet, Forough Farrokhzad

I'm Looking For....

I'm looking for
. . . .
I'm looking for
a person
    a name
        a memory.

I'm looking for
       myself
lost in...

I come from
. . . .
I come from
a city
    a town
        a village
           a street
              a house.

I come from
a house with a
      window
to the sunlight
with a window
looking to sky
    to birds,
        to a river.

I crossed

. . . . . .

I crossed
an ocean
    a sea
      a river.

A river flowing from
           eternity
to eternity.

I sat down
beside the river
and sang a
      song.

The river took
      my song
        my soul

I'm looking for

. . . .

I'm looking for.

~ The Woman and The Mirror ~

He's coming, I hear him braking. I'm sure it's him. The garage door opened. He's coming in. I'm glad he's back. What time is it? Oh my God! A quarter to twelve. I've been sitting in front of the mirror for three hours — no, more — three hours and 45 minutes, since the children went to bed. I didn't even read my book. It's good he's come back home. He's been gone three days. He said he had to go. They are constructing a building up in the north, near the city of Sari. The children and I went there once too. Some enormous building. Only the walls were up then. He said it would take two years to complete.

One year has passed. He goes there every weekend, including long weekends. He says he has to. We all were supposed to go — to the hotel there. It was cosy, clean and near the forest, pleasant. It's only ten minutes away from a village which has a small bazaar. We were very happy when we were there last fall. We haven't been back. The children are going to school and I have to stay with them. Behrooz doesn't ask us to come along anymore. Whenever I mention it, he says, "It's cold, it's raining, you'll be bored." But he goes every week, and every holiday. He says he has to, has to be with his workers.

He comes into the room. I get up but I don't feel like it. I would like to sit in front of the mirror to watch him in it.

So that he can't see me. I want to see how he looks when he comes in. He plays his role very well, thinking I know nothing, but I know everything. Looks calm as he enters. I can't stay in front of the mirror. Damn it. I'm such a coward. When I see him, I feel lost. I want to be pretty, prettier than Soheila — she is beautiful. Damn her. She's beautiful. She's young — not even twenty-two. Her husband was killed in the war last year. She's a slut, but she's beautiful. I met her last year at Mr. Faramarzi's just after her husband's death. Behrooz was there too. Then she came to our home one day and said she was looking for a job. I don't know whether they arranged to meet at Mr. Faramarzi's or later on. I didn't notice anything at first. She started working in Behrooz's office, but she left after two months. When I asked Behrooz's secretary about her, she told me she'd left. They didn't know her phone number. They were probably laughing at me.

Behrooz changes his clothes. I sit on the edge of the bed and ask, "How was the trip?"

He smiles at me, he's a good actor. He says, "I'm tired, don't bother me." He looks indifferent. Sure he's tired, tired of making love for three days in that hotel. The fatigue shows on his face. But he seems younger — more vigorous. He's oblivious to the children and me.

He's gone to the bathroom. I'm still sitting on the edge of the bed. My heart is heavy and beating hard. What am I going to do? Shall I lay down beside him and wait for him to caress me? If he turns his back to me and falls asleep, should I stifle my crying? I'll talk to him. But no, it's not the right time. He's tired, he'll be angry. I'll leave it for tomorrow. I'm not sure what to do. I can't bear his indifference. He loved me until last year. He was eager to make love at any time. But these last eight months he has changed. Lying beside him I don't feel I'm his wife now. He has Soheila,

57

younger and more beautiful than I am. Now he doesn't need me anymore. I'm going to choke with all my tears.

He's back. I wipe the tears away. Why doesn't he look at me? Perhaps he feels ashamed. Shame? No, I can't believe that. If he felt shame, he wouldn't have taken up with Soheila.

He asks why I'm sitting up. I don't answer. He says, "Don't you want to sleep?"

I say, "Yes," and try to smile, but can't.

He asks, "Shall I turn the light off?"

I say, "Yes." He turns it off, and gets into bed. He doesn't ask about the children.

I'm choking with anger and despair. I can't stop these feelings. I want to say, "I'm worth nothing to you, you traded me for Soheila, but what about our children? Do you have new children too?" But it's not possible to have children in eight months. Maybe she's pregnant. My anger is killing me. My heart is beating fast.

Behrooz is fast asleep. I know from his breathing. I wish I had a hammer to crack his skull. If Soheila is pregnant, everything is over. I'll have to put up with her for the rest of my life.

"*Havoo.*" What a disgusting word! A word which never entered my mind. Is it possible? Behrooz? Who pretended to be educated, an intellectual, a man who condemns bigamy?

My pillow is wet from my tears. I wipe them away with the sheet and put it in my mouth to stifle my cries. My tears are the tears of humiliation. Why am I silent? There is no choice, I have to be. What can I do? Where can I find shelter if I leave my home? Should I leave this house which my friends all envy? What about my children, my two sons? I can't do it. I am dependent on this house. Without it I'm nothing. I don't want to be left, drifting in space like a feather!

A divorced woman who has left her home and her children has no place. I must stay. Everything will pass. Eventually Behrooz will tire of Soheila, as he has tired of me. But I... I'm still young, not even thirty years old, and Soheila is twenty-two. Oh my God, how long before she becomes my age! And then I will be forty! All that time I'd have to beg him to love me and he wouldn't. No, I can't do it.

I sob louder and tremble.

My crying wakes Behrooz. He turns on the light. I've covered my face with the sheet. I can't breathe. The anger is like a ball of lead in my chest. Behrooz touches my shoulder, asking, "What's the matter? Are you going crazy again?"

His words cut me like a blade. It's not the first time this has happened. Whenever he goes away for a week and I know that he is going with Soheila I'm beside myself. He caresses me and swears he loves only me. He says he's going for the sake of his job, and I force myself to believe him. His caressing hands soothe me. I try to forget. But then...

This time I don't yield. His caresses and his kisses just annoy me. If Soheila becomes pregnant, I'm sure he'll marry her. I'm depressed. Why do I have to go along with this and be humiliated? He caresses me, but I'm tired — tired of the anger, the resistance and the suffering. It's no use. He says, "Are you going nuts again?"

I want to ask him if Soheila is pregnant, but I don't. This terrible nightmare must never become a reality. I don't want to talk about it. In time everything will pass and I'll have him back for myself again — with all his caresses and his kindness. Talking about it may make it come true. I know it's real, but I'm not going to talk about it. I'll put it out of my mind.

Behrooz says, "You make me tired. You always bother me when I come back home. You're making me nervous."

I stop crying. I would like to forget if only I could. He moves away from me.

I say, "It's not my fault."

He says, "It's your fault. You're stupid."

His insult stings. I shout at him, "I'm not stupid."

He sits down and asks, "What do you want from me?"

I say, "Nothing."

I should be silent. I'm afraid to ask anything else, afraid to make the reality true. What should I do? Live with his bigamy or leave and give up everything? I love this house. I furnished it myself. And what about my children — how can I ever leave my children? The law doesn't let me have custody of them. And even if it did, how could I look after them? Here they have everything they need. It makes Behrooz angry when I stay silent. He lays down angrily, pulling the sheet over himself, and falls asleep. I anxiously wait a few minutes. He doesn't turn back to me.

I've ruined everything. He's humiliated me again and then leaves me alone to weep with my anger and frustration in silence, alone. I get up and leave the bed. I go to the bathroom to sob behind the closed door. I notice my face in the mirror — defeated, not beautiful. I've become old and wrinkled. My eyes are red, my lips are swollen. The tears don't stop when I wash my face. My mouth feels bitter. Frustration makes me think about suicide. I could cut my veins and end this humiliating life. I think of my children again and my tears come faster. I can't do it. I haven't the nerve. I think about leaving him in the morning. This thought seems to open a window for me. But if she's pregnant... There is no choice.

My tears have dried up. There are no more. I stand a long

time and stare at my face — I look wretched. The house is silent. I'm exhausted. My feet are numb. I must go back to our bed and get some sleep. Behrooz will be gone before I wake up. Since I'm not sure about Soheila, I'll stay in this house with my children. This is all I have. Maybe later...

Havoo — co-wife

The Shadows

The shadows — colours
making a mirage in my
                    room.

Each night
I dream
of a happy woman
sitting by her window
singing a song.

Her hands weaving a
                    shawl
her feet waiting in
                    hope
her heart beating with
                    pain.

She is sad — a smile
paints her face
shares life with a stranger
calls him her man.

The shadows — colours
dancing in her house
make a feast of a
                    mirage.

~ Ziba's Portrait ~

It was six months since she had left. She should have left his memory too, but she hadn't. Hormoz sat on the chair and looked around the room. It was a week since he had any money and a job... he had looked for one. He didn't work for a few months; then he found a short-term job and then again — unemployment. Perhaps it was his fault too. He didn't do his best. Since Ziba had left him, it seemed that he had lost something. He was restless.

For three days, he hadn't eaten well; a piece of bread, a sandwich, cheap fruit. His cigarettes were finished too. He got up to look for a cigarette. He searched everywhere; behind the television, between the books, and inside the fridge. Sometimes Ziba put cigarettes in the fridge. He looked under the bed too, but he found nothing.

He sat on a chair, distracted, tired and hungry. His head was empty, or rather full of smoke, full of fog, a heavy fog.

Ziba's portrait on the mirror smiled at him. Ziba had painted the portrait when she went to the painting course. One day she sat in front of the mirror and drew a self-portrait. A portrait of her whole body. The same slender tall body, with tiny fingers. She stared at him, with an indifferent smile. At the beginning, it was not indifferent. It was kind. But in the portrait the smile was cold. The mirror, with its carved wooden frame, was given to Ziba by a friend who was moving to another city. The mirror was expensive.

"I will sell it." He got up, took the mirror off the wall and put it on the floor. Now Ziba looked shorter; she didn't even reach his shoulder. But she still had the same indifferent smile. He sat down again to look at the portrait.

It was six months since she had left. Six months. He thought back. A cold winter day. After a bitter dispute with him, she left. Was it his fault? Perhaps. He didn't know. He didn't want to know. He never liked to think about that. The relationship was like a bubble about to burst. Ziba was patient — at the beginning she was — but then she became impatient. She answered back all his outbursts.

And then...she left him. Her last sentence was, "Living with you makes me crazy."

Hormoz sat on the chair and thought, who was he, to make Ziba crazy? Ziba looked at him indifferently from the mirror. She seemed to lean back into the mirror. Ziba and her portrait had become one. And then...she came alive. Her smile changed. She became gentle. She moved her hands, tossing her long and wavy hair; she wetted her lips with her tongue, her lipstick faded, her earrings fluttered as her body moved. She came out of the mirror and sat on the sofa. The only sofa in the room, with his dirty shirt on it. She took the shirt, put it on the floor and sat down. She put her hands on her knees and spoke. Her voice filled the room, "Do you want to sell me?"

It was not Ziba's portrait that spoke. It was Ziba herself. Hormoz was quiet. Like when Ziba had said, "Let's talk together. We are two mature persons. Mature, wise and educated."

He was stubborn, had cursed her and said, "Damn this education, and this life."

"What do you mean? Which life? This is our life. We made it. We are responsible for it."

When Ziba talked, her logic was strong. She was reasonable. And he could say nothing. Subdued, he accepted her reasons. But...after a few days, something else annoyed him. Was it his fault? He didn't like to think about it.

"You don't want to accept it. Since you are so stubborn and won't give up your high-handed ideas, we can't deal with each other."

He didn't want to give up. Ziba was talking. But she was an easy-going woman. At the beginning she was. She took care of everything; sometimes she got mad and made a lot of fuss about a shirt on the sofa, or an unwashed plate on the table, or the burned teapot left on the stove without water. She got mad at every little thing. The home atmosphere became heavy.

"These trivial things make up life. Life is a collection of these things, and talking..."

"Why are you talking so rudely? Think about what you are going to say. Accept that I'm a human being like you. I have the same abilities that you have. Accept that I'm the same as you are."

He had to sit and think about that. He loved Ziba. Ziba handled the house and worked outside too. But why didn't he want to accept that she was the same as he was? He didn't listen to her.

"Listen, I'm talking to you. Why don't you listen to me? You make me crazy with your behaviour. My patience has run out." It was over. She left.

It was six months since she had left. He didn't go to bring her back. He was thinking there were so many Zibas. And now...six months had passed. Ziba's portrait had taken Ziba's place. Whenever he was home, he sat in front of Ziba's portrait and she talked to him as if she were with him. She talked about everyday things, life, the street, friends, shopping, the weather, the biting cold. Ziba's portrait had taken the place of Ziba herself. Now Ziba's portrait sat on the sofa and asked him, "Do you want to sell me?"

He looked at her. Did he love her? He didn't know. He got Ziba very easily. Like something on sale. When she said, "I'm leaving," he didn't believe it. No, she would not leave. She loved him. She was dependent on him. He remembered the first months of their marriage; she loved him so much, like a bird in love.

"Have you ever been in love?"

Love? He didn't know. He didn't know love. But he loved Ziba.

"I know I love you."

"No, you don't. I don't believe that you love me. Your love is not love."

What happened to Ziba's love?

"My love disappeared. Like water evaporated on a summer's day. It's gone up to the sky, never to come back, it's gone."

Ziba's portrait got up impatiently, and stood in the mirror frame again and didn't ask anymore, "Do you want to sell me?"

I have to sell it, he thought. He was dizzy. He hadn't eaten for a few days, nor smoked, nor drank alcohol. His head was as empty as a drum. His stomach became so small he could crumple it up and throw it away. He wished he could do that and make himself free. Free of everything, of a brain, stomach, heart. Heart? Did he have one?

Ziba used to say, "You don't have a heart. You don't understand the meaning of love."

He didn't. He didn't learn to understand, but he had an ego. His ego was enormous. "Your ego will kill you."

Now his ego shouted at him, "Sell it. Don't be happy with a portrait. With Ziba gone, what is the use of her portrait? There are so many Zibas."

Was it true? Were there so many? No, he didn't believe it. In these six months he hadn't met any Zibas. Ziba was right.

"Nobody can put up with you. Nobody can tolerate your meaningless ego. Break it. Shatter it. Free yourself from it."

He couldn't. He was raised with an ego. He got his identity from his ego. He was a man, after all!

He got tired of so many disturbing thoughts. Ziba's portrait with her indifferent, even loathing smile, looked at him.

"Do what you want to do. Make your decision. Why have you become so undecided?"

He was spineless. Ziba had taken his strength. In these six months, he had no life. He was like a feather drifting in space; he could not stay at home or go out. He didn't know what he was looking for. He was not looking for Ziba. If he was, he could go and bring her back.

"No, let her go. I don't want her any more. There are so many Zibas."

But he hasn't met any Zibas.

Hormoz got up. He had to sell it. He needed the money. He knew that he would get good money for it. The antique seller who was their friend had told him that both the frame and the portrait were expensive.

At the shop he put the mirror on the counter and opened the paper around it.

"Do you want to sell it?" the shop owner asked.

Hormoz nodded.

"Are you sure that you want to sell it?" he repeated.

He didn't answer. He stared at the owner's face.

"Have you thought about it?"

"Yes," he said angrily. "I need the money."

Hormoz took the money and put it in his pocket. The shop owner put the mirror on the counter and looked at it with admiration. He held both sides of the frame and stared at the portrait.

As Hormoz went out the door, he turned back. Ziba's portrait with that indifferent smile seemed to be saying, "At last you sold me, but it's not important. I have a place here, but you... Where do you go?"

When Hormoz crossed the street he thought he saw Ziba moving through the crowd. A feeling of joy mixed with remorse filled his heart. He abruptly turned back. He decided to get back Ziba's portrait and then to ask Ziba to come back. He had to tell her, "I love you. I love you with all my soul."

And she would come back. She would certainly come back.

A sound of a car brake echoed in the street. The mirror fell out of the shop-owner's hands and shattered into a thousand pieces. He crossed the street and followed Ziba as she walked away. Calling her name, he ran to reach her. She turned back around and looked at him with surprise. The woman was not Ziba.

Ziba — female Iranian name meaning beautiful.

This is Me

My story is blank
my story is untold.

When you pass by a small
                    house
light in the window
listen to my song.

The song was sung
before I was born
a song of
              solitude.

In my little world
are too many tales for
                narrating.

When you pass by my
              house
just knock at the door
a woman is waiting
with a broken
              heart
with an old book
              on her lap
with an aged child crying
              on her back.

A woman with a sad
                    story
me.

~ Deliriously Happy ~

He had come to pick me up, like other nights. Like other nights when I left the Donut Shop, the pure dawn cold slapped my face. Sharp as a knife's blade, but fresh. It washed my body, as if I had taken a cold shower. Shivering, I reached the taxi. Inside, it was warm with the familiar smell of Parviz's body, the taste of cigarette smoke on his lips.

"You're frozen!"

He drove.

"How was business?"

"Wonderful! I had two wealthy passengers who were leaving for Florida. One of them was by himself, plump and big and a face like a red watermelon, shining with happiness. He was going to join his girlfriend. Two weeks vacation lying in sunshine on the beach with its greenish water, under wild palms and blue sky. A real paradise! And the other one was with his family. They all had blond hair like cornflower. Two handsome boys, like apples, white and red and happy. They talked nonstop. They entertained me too. I said, Don't forget a gift for me, a dish full of sunshine! They laughed. And the man gave me fifty bucks. Didn't take the change. The other one was happy too. He wasn't married, didn't have children. But he had a good business. He gave me fifty bucks too, and didn't take back the change. If only I had such passengers every night!"

Parviz was happy, deliriously happy. He had two wealthy passengers. He got a good tip. I was happy too. That night I didn't have too many customers. Perhaps the cold weather had sent the late night drunks to their houses. I had a chance to sit and watch the street.

The street slid away under the taxi. Shops were closed. The snow was shovelled in front of the houses and the shops. The street was neat, sliding away under the taxi. A TTC bus roared uphill. We passed it. There were only a few passengers in it.

"Recite me a poem."

He recited from the well-known poets Sepehri, Shamloo, Forough and Hafez.

"Recite me one of your poems."

"Don't talk about that."

"Why? I love your poetry. I was your beloved in those poems. Was it me? Was it really me? I don't believe it."

"Yes it was you. Why don't you believe it? In the days when I first met you."

"In the preparation course, do you remember? I was studying to pass the university entrance exam. And I met you."

"I didn't let you study. I plucked you off your life's tree like a ripe fruit."

"And I grew with you, and bore fruit."

"Yes, I left a baby in your lap. And you couldn't study anymore. And then exile."

"And now I have you. I have Ramin. I am happy."

"But it's a struggle. Night work, I know it's hard for you. You shouldn't work. It's not right to leave the child alone at home. A ten-year-old child, like Ramin, so fearful. It's not right. And you want to study."

"I'm studying. You see that I'm studying. I'll finish a few

years later. It's not a problem. I can't bear to see you work seventeen or eighteen hours a day."

"We didn't have to buy this house."

"But we bought it. It will be hard for a few years, then it will be over. It will not be forever."

"Who knows how long our lives will go on."

"No, don't talk like that. I help you. I work nights. Ramin won't wake up. He sleeps heavily. Even if there's a cannon shot, he won't wake up. He doesn't know when I leave or when I come back. He hasn't woken up during these past six months."

"But it's better to tell him. If he finds out he's alone at home, he will die of fright. We have to tell him."

"No, it's better for him to know nothing."

Parviz drove, humming quietly. I put my head on his shoulder. With closed eyes I saw the street slide away under the taxi and disappear. At 30 below zero the street looked vulnerable. The shops were closed and lights showed their goods in the windows. The houses, with closed doors and silent windows, continued on with their night's dreams. And I was thinking of home! A weekend, to sleep beside Parviz, until noon, or even later. Ramin would sleep too. He wouldn't wake up until I called him. And Parviz was happy. He was humming, reciting poems. He kissed my hair. He was not in a bad mood like other nights.

"How are you darling?" he asked me.

"Good! I had some big customers. Just a few. Tonight was quiet. I had time to sit and rest. An hour ago, a bunch of old men and women came in. They ate well and left a good tip for me too. They were not like other people who give just a nickel or a dime. I had a good night tonight. If only every night..."

"If every night was like tonight..."

"Would you write poetry again?"

"Don't talk about that subject. Forget that I was ever a poet."

"I loved you because of those poems. I was your beloved in those poems. Wasn't I?"

"You still are."

"So, why don't you write poetry anymore?"

"I will. One day when I get rid of those mortgages, the mortgage on the house, the mortgage on the taxi. That's the day I'll start again."

"That's the day the house will be ours, and you will plant vegetables and flowers in the garden. And I'll finish school, get a good job, Ramin will start university, and you'll write poetry again."

"Talk about something else. Forget about poetry."

"What should I talk about? I like to talk about good things, beautiful things."

"Wouldn't you like to invite your parents? Don't you miss them?"

"Why shouldn't I? I miss them a lot. But it's not possible at the moment. You know that too. So why do we talk about it?"

"But you can wish it. We can talk about our wishes. One day when our mortgage is paid, we will invite them. Your parents and my mother... All of them. How's that?"

"And my little sister will come here to go to ballet school. You know how she longed to be a ballerina. I can still remember her, always in front of the mirror, dancing like she was on stage."

"And my sister will come here to continue her studies."

"Yes, I remember she liked astronomy."

"When we lived in Kerman, at night, she always used to look at the clear desert sky. She knew a lot about the stars... And your brother."

"But he can't. He's prohibited from leaving the country. You know that."

"I know, but when the time comes, I hope he won't have any problems."

"And your brother too."

"You know that nobody can make him move."

"But when all of them want to come, he'll come too."

"All of them together! If they won't give them visas?"

"Perhaps they would. If we had enough money, good jobs, they would."

I kissed Parviz. I was so happy, I was floating. Was it possible? Maman and Baba. Nasrin and Naser, all of them together! Like when we were in Iran.

"Why can't it be possible? Everything is possible in this world. If every night I could have such rich passengers in good moods, who have many credit cards and fifty-dollar bills lying side-by-side in their wallets, who give fifty-dollar bills and don't want change. If I get those passengers every night, the house mortgage will soon be paid and you won't have to work."

"But I'm working to finish the mortgage on the taxi, and you shouldn't have to work seventeen or eighteen hours a day. You come back home late at night tired and in a bad mood and I don't dare ask you to recite a poem for me."

"I told you not to talk about this subject."

"Why? I love your poetry. I'm your beloved in your poetry."

"Now you're just my real-life beloved."

He kissed me. The taste of cigarette was on his lips. And

75

I was dreaming about sleeping. My body didn't listen to me and was falling asleep. Drowsy, I leaned my head on Parviz's shoulder. My eyes were closed by the time we reached home.

I opened the door. Parviz parked the taxi and I got out. I opened the front door as Parviz reached it. I saw him first. I screamed. Parviz ran to Ramin. He sat on the stairs in the front hall, his head leaning on the wall.

I explained to the doctor that Ramin never wakes up during the night. He sleeps heavily. I always have difficulty in waking him up in the mornings. He makes me crazy. When he falls asleep, he doesn't wake up even if there are drums. He sleeps like a log. I was pretty certain he wouldn't wake up.

Ramin talked deliriously, unaware of what he was saying, something meaningless. He stared at us as if he didn't know us.

"What happened to him?" I asked the doctor.

"Shock," the doctor said. "He is in shock. It may take sometime to recover. You should be patient."

~ Lover of Humankind ~

When the telephone rang Manijeh answered. After hello and the usual conversation, she was silent, just listening. Karim watched as Manijeh hugged her knees in contemplation, oblivious to her surroundings. It was not clear whether she was listening or thinking. She seemed stunned. Then she murmured, "You're right. We have to do something."

Yoosef asked, "Who are you talking to?"

Manijeh didn't hear him. She was still listening on the phone. Then she put down the receiver and looked at her friends who were watching her, except for Maliheh who was turning pages in a magazine.

Manijeh regained herself. Still hugging her knees, she said, "Soraya was on the phone. Her mother had a heart attack and was taken to the hospital. Soraya spent last night and today with her, but tonight she has to go to work. You know, she works the night shift and can't leave her job. She wanted to know if one of us could volunteer to stay with her mother for a night."

There was silence for a minute. Maliheh continued leafing through the magazine. Karim, peeling an orange, slowly looked away from Manijeh, from Yoosef to Kaveh. He expected that everyone would rush to help. Each one waited for the other to come forward. Still sitting on the floor,

Manijeh stretched out her legs; she put the telephone on her knees, as if to dial a number.

There was a long silence. They all looked at each other. Manijeh, like a teacher scolding her students, said, "Why don't you say something? One of us should help her. She is alone. Her mother arrived from Tehran just three weeks ago — after five years she has come to see her daughter. And suddenly she is sick and taken to the hospital. Soraya said she's in critical condition and is in the ICU. She's very frightened and doesn't like Soraya to leave her alone, but Soraya has to go to work, otherwise she'll lose her job."

There was silence again. Maliheh idly turned the pages of the magazine. Karim looked around at everyone, then gazed at Maliheh. Maliheh returned his look for a few seconds. It was clear she was the only one who could spend a few nights with Soraya's mother. She didn't have to worry about losing her job or taking care of a small baby. But Karim looked away from her to Manijeh and said,

"I hope you don't volunteer. You know Damon can't sleep without you. And your headache will come back and you'll be in pain again."

Manijeh agreed. "Me? How can I stay awake the whole night? You know very well that lack of sleep makes me ill, I'd have to pay for weeks."

Karim said, "It's a good thing you're thinking about that, otherwise you would be the first person offering to help."

"Why shouldn't I be?" Manijeh said. "What good is friendship if I couldn't help at such a difficult time? I wouldn't be a friend. But what can I do? This is out of my hands. Damon doesn't sleep without me and I will have to suffer for several weeks. But, one sleepless night never killed anyone."

Maliheh looked up from the magazine, "If her mother is

in the ICU, then why does she need someone? There are nurses. Hospitals here are not like those in Iran where no one cares about the patient."

"Who says so?" Yoosef responded. "Here it's no better than Iran. I think over there the nurses and doctors are more caring."

"It's not a question of caring," Manijeh said. "The problem is that her mother doesn't know a word of English, and she's frightened to be in hospital. Soraya said she was frightened to be in hospital in Iran too. But here it's worse. I have to give Soraya an answer. She is calling me back for our decision. She called several friends — Ashraf, Rahim, and Mrs. Yasaie — but they weren't home. She thought of me. But I really don't know what to do. Her mother's an old woman who needs help. She has come to see her daughter after five years of being apart, and instead she has to stay in the hospital. If we don't help her now, when can we? But, anyway I can't do it. If I don't sleep for just one night my headache and nightmares will be back. And what can I do with Damon? If he wakes up in the middle of the night and doesn't see me, he'll never stop crying."

Manijeh turned to Maliheh, "What about you Maliheh?"

Maliheh reddened. She was silent and then said, "I have to be at work at six o'clock. My work is not easy. I have responsibilities. I have to open the store." Without looking at anybody she continued, "I'm sure you know I can't stand insomnia. And Soraya doesn't have a good relationship with me. Have you forgotten about Bahman? She thought I took him from her. You all know what kind of person he is! I wasn't guilty. Bahman and I went to a movie once, and she made a lot of trouble about that. But I was lucky — I got to know his character by going to one movie with him. He was talking behind Soraya's back. I don't want to repeat his foolish words.

"But you, Manijeh you know very well what Soraya said about me. Now, how do you expect me to go to the hospital and take care of her mother? I didn't even know when her mother came from Iran. Last week she invited all of you. Well, she was right in not inviting me, it's been a long time since we talked to each other. She was a nice girl. I respected her, especially when we were in Iran. Now she's another person. People seem to change.

"In Iran her eldest brother helped me very much. He found someone to help me to escape from Iran. But Soraya herself was not good to me. I'll never forget what she did to me as long as I live. I wouldn't have known her so well if it wasn't for the Bahman incident. Now I can't forget what happened. Her mother is a good woman. I've been in her home many times, but on top of everything else, I'm not someone who can stand insomnia. And I can't stand the hospital atmosphere. And my English is not very good. And since she's in the ICU, there's no need for extra help."

Manijeh waited with the telephone on her knees.

Kaveh said, "I am ready to go. I know Soraya, she is a good person. She's kind and generous. Whenever I needed help, she gave it to me. But what can I do about my wife? My wife is afraid to stay alone. You know we live in a bad neighbourhood. In that basement, I'm afraid to be alone too. Since there was the break-in and an old woman was killed, Farzaneh doesn't want to be home alone, even briefly during the day. When her class finishes, she goes to the library and waits for me to bring her home."

"Bring Farzaneh over here," Manijeh said. "Let her stay with us tonight."

"With you?" Kaveh exclaimed.

"Yes," Manijeh said. "What is the matter with that?"

Kaveh pondered the suggestion. "I don't think it's possible. She is at Nahid's right now. You know where she lives, quite far from here. If I go and bring her here, it will be ten o'clock. Then, when do I go to hospital? Which hospital is it anyway?"

"I didn't ask her," Manijeh said. "When she calls again, she'll tell me."

Karim looked at Yoosef, "What about you. Do you have a problem too?"

"My problem is something else," Yoosef said.

"He can't do such a thing," Manijeh said.

Kaveh said, "Yes, I told Yoosef so many times to give up his drug addiction. He doesn't care. He only wants to escape from this world." He turned to Yoosef, "You used to talk all the time about humankind. You loved to be with people. Why have you withdrawn from others now? Change your life and live like a decent person. How long do you think you will live? I feel sorry for you, having such a shabby life. Look at you, an engineer, first-class student at university. What happened to you? Why do you put yourself down? People should be competing to hire you."

"I've applied for so many jobs and didn't get any," Yoosef said. "We are nothing in this country. You know better than I about this. What are you doing now? You are just an assembly worker, tightening screws. Is that what you're worth? You once flew across the sky and hated to put your feet on the ground! Flying used to be your passion!"

"Why are you talking so much about yourselves and your past?" Manijeh said. "Think about Soraya. She's in a desperate situation. Her mother has had a heart attack and is in critical condition. Soraya herself has to go to work without having slept last night. And tonight she has to deal with all those night owls in that filthy donut shop and if she doesn't go to work she will lose her job. Think about that poor girl."

"Soraya has high hopes," Maliheh said. "Here, nobody thinks about such matters. It's hard even for anybody to deal with his own problems. Remember the time I had the appendicitis operation. Nobody asked about me."

And then she looked at Manijeh, "Just you came to see me."

"You are so ungrateful," Yoosef said. "You said that Nastran and Nahid had come to visit you."

Maliheh said, "Yes — for one second and then they left."

"You say in this country everyone should pull their own *gilim* out of the river," Karim said. "So, why do you expect anything from others?"

"In this country everyone should stretch out on the ground and expire. Let's all do it together," Kaveh said.

Manijeh put the telephone on the floor, sat beside Karim on the sofa and said, "I feel sorry for all of us. I want to cry."

The telephone rang. Karim took the receiver. Soraya's sobbing could be heard.

Karim asked with a hesitant voice, "When did it happen?"

They all avoided each other's eyes. Manijeh stared at the bare window covered by dark night.

gilim — A cheap handmade rug

~ Hands ~

The street was a roaring monster. Cars passed
incessantly, black, grey, white, red, small, big. Layla looked
at the cars, but not one of them looked back. The windows
were up as they sped by. As she reached the intersection,
the light turned red and she stopped. The cars accelerated
and passed quickly by.

Layla stood for a while, her hands weighed down. Pain
reached from her shoulder to her elbows. The light remained
red, cars tore past. She put the bags in her left hand down
on the wet ground, her fingers still on the handles. If she let
go of the bags, it would not be easy to collect them again.
She remained bent over, ignoring the weight of the bags,
opened and closed her fingers around the handles. People
around her started to walk as the light turned green. Layla
lifted the bags. Pain crawled into her hands like a serpent.
She gazed at the cars — at the men and women in them,
calm and quiet, staring into the distance, seat belts tightened,
feet on the brakes, ready to drive.

The street was so wide that just as she reached the traffic
island, the light turned amber. Layla stopped. If she didn't
have the bags, she would have made it. With the bags it was
impossible. She set them down, but didn't leave them. She
stayed bent over holding onto the handles. When she opened
her fingers they were numb. There was no one else on the

island, everyone else had crossed over. She stood — two heavy loads hanging from her shoulders. Cars passed by. Layla calculated the distance across the intersection and from the curb to her building.

Layla was half-way across. She could see the building, but it was far away. "I shouldn't buy so much," she thought. "I'll get myself killed."

The light turned green. Layla crossed slowly and deliberately. The cars were stopped in a row. She looked at them — men, women, old and young, quiet and indifferent. Layla wished she could throw all her bags at them, but she kept going with shoulders down and tortured fingers. She crossed slowly. "If only I didn't have to shop at the discount store!"

Layla reached the other curb. Pain spread from her spine to her waist. But she had to keep going. Her building was in view. The road was uphill. Loaded down, Layla carried on. A young white girl rushed by and left her far behind. Her feet clung to the ground. Layla was moving slower and slower. "Thank God — there is no intersection."

The wind lashed her, but Layla didn't feel it. She was hot and sweaty. The pain was overwhelming. She couldn't endure any more and put the bags on a bench. Traffic roared by. Layla felt a scream build up in her. The wind beat Layla's body and dried the sweat. She shivered. She liked sitting on the bench, but the wind forced her on. Layla took the bags once more.

"If only I could see a friend," Layla thought. There were no pedestrians, only cars and tall buildings. Layla recalled her small home town with rows of houses and friendly twisting alleyways — destroyed by the war now — and its inhabitants long fled.

Layla, lifted the bags, took a deep breath and set off,

taking a few quick steps, then slowing down again. Layla seemed to have lost strength, only ten steps and she felt she was going to collapse. She put the bags down, hunched over. Her hands felt as if they were falling off. Layla gazed at the building ahead — high, white with windows lit up. So far off, it seemed to be standing an eternity away. "I must reach it," she thought.

She lifted the bags and rushed ahead. A young Black couple passed her, holding hands. Layla wanted to ask them for a hand, but they had already passed. Layla felt helpless, the distance was too great. Though her building was the closest, it seemed miles away. She thought back to the city where she was born, the people there and how on days when she had a heavy load to carry, there were always friends around to help her carry it.

Layla saw no one in the street. And if she had, it was bound to be a stranger. Nothing but the building and the cars passing by, oblivious to her.

Layla put the bags down again and waited. She had made it more than halfway home travelling by two buses and a train, but what was left seemed even longer. Now night was falling on the street, only the cars' bright eyes pierced the darkness. Time stood still. Fatigue was crushing her. The futility of struggling cast a shadow over her. It was as if she was walking in empty space. The high buildings seemed to be in a haze. The one where Layla lived receded farther and farther away.

Layla regained composure. She was still conscious, but dead tired. Lifting the bags again, this time Layla didn't hurry, just took her time. She knew that every step would bring her closer to her building and this knowledge pushed her ahead. Layla felt the pain less and less as she walked on. And now she could see her entrance door, just as a woman entered carrying some bags. Probably she had shopped at the store near by. "If I had shopped there I would be back too, but the prices are twice as high and I couldn't afford to buy half as many things," Layla thought, and wished she had bought half as much.

She figured she could reach the door in just a few minutes. It wasn't hazy there. Her building loomed in front of her — the entrance door with its huge windows and the building number beside it. But her arms were pulling out of their sockets. Layla put her bags down again, soaked with sweat. She couldn't move on — pain seeped through her waist, down into her feet.

Layla saw a man entering the building and thought, "If I could get over there, he could hold it open for me. That's the only thing I can expect from anyone."

Then a young man appeared from the other side to enter the building. He saw her. "He might help me," Layla thought. But he went on by her and into the building. She lifted the bags. Now she was no more than fifteen steps from her building. At the entrance she transferred all the bags to one hand and pushed open the heavy door with the other. Layla looked behind her and couldn't see anyone to help her. She felt that her arms had separated from her shoulders. She was going to faint. Her hands were numb. She opened the door and went inside. Layla had no further to go, just the elevator and then her apartment. She rode up, staggered into her kitchen and set the bags down. Removing her coat and her boots, she laid down on her bed and breathed deeply. The sweat evaporated from her body. With her hands folded across her chest, she could hear her heart pounding. Her hands rested, crossed on her chest. She felt sympathy for them. In this harsh world, they were her only true friends.

Man or Woman

At last I saw you
                    today
five years
day by day
night by night
a wall between
                    us.

Our running water
our bath shower
our TV
humming together.

At last I saw you
                    today
carried down
under the ground
an "ah" in my mouth
a question in my mind

old or young
man or woman?

~ A Live Person ~

Hasti asked, "Do you know what I am?"

"What?" Farzaneh answered.

Hasti said, "A live person."

Farzaneh looked at her with astonishment. What else would she be? She's not an animal, or a monster, she's a live person, for sure.

"Don't look at me like that," Hasti said. "I am a live person. I have an identity, a soul, thoughts, a heart, feelings, and I suffer because of my heart and my feelings. I wish I had none of them."

"Then you would not be a live person," Farzaneh said.

"But I am a live person, with all the characteristics of a live person," Hasti continued. "I breathe, eat, sleep and work. Yes, in fact, I work like a machine. I work without rest, without greasing, without changing spare parts. I'm forever working."

Hasti talked nonstop. She was not talking to Farzaneh, she was talking to herself. She always talked to herself. Like someone who had multiple personalities. There was always someone else with her who listened to her endless talk. She was a quiet person. But when she started to talk, nobody could stop her. She talked and didn't let Farzaneh open her mouth. She read the questions in Farzaneh's mind and answered them.

"I'm a live person," she said. "Every morning I'm awakened by the radio at a set time. It's an interesting invention. No more being shocked awake by the alarm clock. Now, when I open my eyes, the radio announcer speaks about news or weather with her lovely voice. I find out what is going on in the world, what the temperature is, whether it's snowing or raining, windy or calm.

"I should get up. Words and the sounds prod my body like needles. My brain fills with sounds and words, and the day is on the threshold of birth like a baby. I have no choice, I must get up and start my day. Yes, the day has started — even though the night is still sitting at the window. When I open my eyes, I sense the clouds behind the window. It seems it's snowing. I can't see the snow, but I can guess, it must be snowing when the sky is so cloudy and the clouds are so bright. I have no choice. The day is going to be born. I have to help her. Warmth has stuck to my body like beach sand. I'd like to stay in bed and enjoy its warmth. But it's not possible. Moments pass in silence. I look at the clock radio, ridiculing me and saying, 'Ha? Don't you want to go to work? Aren't you afraid of being laid off? What about your employer's disapproval? Customers' impatience? The long lineup?' Oh, no, I can't quit work, the job was so hard to find. I should get up. Brush away the sleeping sand from my body. Get out of bed, I have forty-five minutes to take a bath, get dressed, have my breakfast, make a sandwich for my lunch."

Farzaneh laughed.

"Are you laughing?" Hasti asked. "Are you surprised? No, it's neither funny, nor surprising. I must be quick. I have to take my lunch too. Should I eat in a restaurant or in a snack bar?"

"Either one," Farzaneh said.

"No, I can't." Hasti said. "I work, I have the right to a hot meal for lunch. But how much do you think a hot lunch costs?"

"It's not very expensive."

"Yes I know, a sandwich, soup and a drink cost almost four or five dollars. It's not a lot of money. But for me it's too much. It's equal to my hourly wage. So it's better not to talk about it. I better take my sandwich with me. You can't compare the prices. There is too much difference. Don't worry, these things are not important. Maybe in the future, when I get a raise, I would like to spend my lunchtime in restaurants or snack bars, have a hot meal and watch those rushing and ambitious people who get lost every morning in office towers and factories all around the city and then emerge at lunch time looking for soup, hamburgers and salad.

"After swallowing the last bite of my breakfast, I put on my boots, my coat, and wrap a scarf around my neck several times. I put on my gloves in the elevator. Then I find myself in the street. It's winter. The weather is cold and the ground is icy. I have to walk fast to catch the bus. But I'm afraid of falling. I walk slowly. The sky is bright. The ground is covered with a delicate layer of snow. The wind blows snow in my face. The street is empty. Cars pass occasionally with their windows up. I don't look at cars. I don't like to look at them. I look for a bus stop at the intersection. I'm worried the bus will be late. I always have to wait a few minutes for the bus. The cold I've felt since leaving home penetrates my coat, my scarf, my boots and my gloves and takes over my body. I feel frozen. My feet are numb, my ears are burning. The wind howls. It seems to be speaking about hungry timber wolves to us, the bus passengers.

"The bus arrives. How slow these people are. They don't

hurry to get into the bus. They board one by one. I get in too, finally. I look for a place to sit, but all the seats are taken and people are quiet, thoughtful, drowsy. I look at them. This is the only time I can observe people. How can I look at people's faces at work? Are the prices of the items written on their faces? If I were a social worker and people came to talk about their problems, I would let them sit and talk about anything while I stare at them, just pretending to listen to them.

"But look, I'm digressing from my daily schedule. There isn't an empty seat on the bus. I have to stand. I hold on to the bar in the bus and stand. I don't see the street, since the windows are blocked by people. Everywhere I look, I see lively and happy people, men and women. The East Asian woman beside me is fast asleep. Another man sitting further away, where could he be from? I can't guess. He is sleeping too. The bus is a good place for sleeping. One can sleep in it standing or sitting. Take for example this old Hindu woman standing beside me. What a braid she has. Shows from under her purple scarf. She has a beauty spot on her nose. She is asleep too. She sometimes opens her eyes and looks around with a start. No, she isn't looking at anything in particular, her eyes just seem to be turning in their sockets — she seems to be dreaming. You see, it's amazing. People sleep in different ways, sitting and standing.

"The minutes in a bus are useless. I have to change from the bus and catch the train. The buses aren't direct. Does this bring me to work? Don't worry. Many people transfer from bus to train! I do too. People walk very fast in subway passages as if they are being followed or are running to win a lottery ticket. I walk fast too. I like mixing with people. Am I joking? It's true. When you see people going somewhere you want to follow them, even though you don't know their destination, or why they are running to get there. At least the good thing is that you get to your destination sooner. On the subway platforms the wind slaps you and wakes you up. I go down the escalator. The station is crowded. I see only people and the two black tunnels that never end. I wait for the train. It comes roaring in and stops. It swallows all the people, men, women, young and old. What luck — an empty seat! I sit. What a pleasure! And the train is warm. However I smell the odours: the smell of celery, garlic, fried onions, perfumes and, worst of all, a person sitting beside me with his mouth open. You laugh! Haven't you ever travelled by train?

"These travelling times usually are useless. But for that I have a plan. I study English, underlining the difficult words. I kill two birds with one stone. I enjoy while learning. At the next station more people come in, adding their smells. But none of this keeps me from sleep, which runs in my veins like blood. Oh silly me. I feel as though I have taken some sleeping tablets. The book I was holding has dropped out of my hands. My eyelids feel stuck. The scream of the train is terrible — like a thousand people screaming together. I open my eyes. People around me sleep or stare into space. The girl opposite is reading with a walkman in her ears. What a lucky person! I read too, but I dream — disturbing dreams about nothing. The screams accumulate in my head. The train stops. I arrive at my destination. My destination? No, the train's destination. I have to take another bus. I wait at the bus stop — new smells. The bus stop, old and cold smells of lingering exhaust fumes and gasoline. You laugh! Doesn't cold have a smell? Cold has a voice too. Cold breathes too. People crowd onto the bus when it comes out of the darkness. The station ceiling is low, forcing the air current to bite my skin like hundreds of bees. The bus is like a big bag, it lets in everyone. But I can't find a place to sit. I arrive at work, standing. Commuting is such a waste of time. Are you laughing? You are right. I repeat it several times. But it's not just talk, it's a fact. Every day, three hours, it's not a short time. But I have a plan for it. I work on my English, sorry that there's no seat for me on the bus.

"Yes, I arrive at work on time and I work like a machine without stopping. How many customers do I have? How many items can I sell? How much money can I make? I don't count — there's no time to count. Sometimes I think about the evening, at home after work — dinner, resting, reading and listening to music. Yes I enjoy reading and listening to music, like a live person. At last work is finished and I am free. Are you laughing? It's true. Finishing work means freedom. I am tied to the cash register and then I'm free. I'm so tired. Are you surprised? Shouldn't I be tired? I have been on my feet for eight hours. Why are you in such a hurry? I'm going home. I have to go back the same way. Oh, home, what a wonderful place! The place for resting and enjoying life. The sink is full of dishes. The kitchen floor is a mess and the living room untidy. I have to keep calm, not scream at the children, not worry about anything. I need to rest first. To rest? How? It's impossible? If I put my head on the pillow, I'll sleep through until morning. What about dinner? The dishes? Besides that, I ought to read and listen to music — the real pleasures of my life. I wash the dishes. I cook the food. I have my dinner. I wash the dishes again. It's ten o'clock. I turn on the TV. I lean my head on the sofa and listen to the news. Reporters talk from around the world. The words make an impression on my brain, but the sentences are not clear. I'm enveloped by a cloud of sleep. I'm swallowed up by the clouds. Sleep carries me away. You laugh. You're right. It's past eleven. Someone calls my name.

It's my daughter. While I change my clothes to go to bed, I ask myself: What kind of person am I?

"And someone screams inside me: 'A live person.'"

Hasti — female Iranian name meaning life
Farzaneh — female Iranian name meaning wisdom

~ A Prayer in the Night ~

The whole day I sat at the window and watched the snow. From the tenth floor, it looked so beautiful. As usual, I was depressed. It's not something new for me to be depressed. I've felt down since the minute I set foot in this country, I can't help myself. I tell myself, "What's wrong with you? You have your life here. You have everything here. Marzieh works all day long, and whenever she takes you to those big stores, she tells you — 'Buy anything you need. Don't stint on anything.'"

I don't. I wander through those spacious stores. How many different cans and jars are there? I don't buy them. How do I know what's in them? I buy fruit, meat, milk. But I feel so down. When I look at all those nice meats, I remember Rafat. She was pregnant when I left her. She must have given birth by now. I know she can't afford to buy meat illegally. With her teacher's pay, and her husband laid off, how she can afford to buy everything that she needs? They were happy just to buy rationed meat. She always looked so pale. Sometimes I gave some of my coupons to them. Even the coupons were bargained illegally.

Here, we have meat or chicken for our meal every day. There's a lot of chicken here. But back there Rafat had to go for it in the early morning and stay in line for hours. Mortaza wouldn't go. He felt ashamed. Sometimes I wish they could come here too. But no, I don't want that. I wish Marzieh and I could go back to our home. Sometimes I wonder why I came here. But I know I came because of Marzieh. That Mrs. Mehrabi wrote me a letter, telling me that my daughter is going to wither away. Marzieh's been here two years now and I thought she would be happy here. And now I wonder why she isn't.

I helped her to escape. The night the guards surrounded our house and rushed in to arrest Marzieh, she was in her room, upstairs.

"Don't come in," I yelled. "I'm naked. Give me two minutes, I'll get dressed."

In those two minutes I went upstairs and told her, "Run away." She escaped through a door in the roof.

Then I put on my *chador*, and went downstairs. My heart was pounding so hard, it felt as if it was in my mouth. I sat on the front stoop and cried loudly. What a noise! I couldn't help it. I was really screaming.

"Damn this situation which has left us with nothing," I cried. "It made my child run away from home. It took my son from me. It took my daughter from me. I have no one. I don't have any children for my old age."

I cried so hard, one of guards felt sorry for me. He had tears in his eyes, and said, "Mother, we have nothing against you, we are looking for your daughter, Marzieh."

"Damn Marzieh," I said. "She's not my daughter any longer. There is no more Marzieh. I took away the name I gave her. I sent her out of my home. She's disgraced me in front of the neighbours." It seemed that they believed me when I cursed Marzieh.

Later, Marzieh told me she had heard everything I said. Yes, I let her escape like that. Then she couldn't come back home any more. I sent her to the north of the city to my brother's house. She was there for a week. But my nephew found out that the revolutionary guards were following her and he sent her away, out into the night. She came back home, and said, "I have to leave the country."

I don't know how she got out of the country. She never told me anything. I didn't have any news from her for months. I suffered a lot. Then one day she called me. When I heard her voice, it was as if I had arisen from the dead. I love Marzieh in a way I can't explain. She was two years old when her father died. I raised her by myself. She had a special love for me and she still has. I think she was depressed because she was so far away from me. If kind Mrs. Mehrabi didn't write me about her, how would I know what was happening? Marzieh didn't write me one word. She always wrote, "I'm okay."

But after two years when I saw her, I didn't recognize her. Not because I didn't recognize my own child. It was Marzieh. But what a change! She had become old, very old. She seemed confused. Then, after a few days, when she believed I was really there, she asked me, "Is our house still there? The yard, the pond, and the Plane tree. Do you remember how shady it was? I used to take a nap in its shade on a summer afternoon and you would yell at me, 'You will get a headache.' But I didn't care. I liked the sound of leaves whispering. It seemed that they told me a tale."

At the beginning I couldn't help crying. Marzieh asked me, "What's the matter Maman. Why are you crying?"

"Nothing," I said. "I feel sad, I think I'm homesick."

"Don't talk about sadness," she said. "The longer you stay, the more you feel it."

It's five months since I've been here. Marzieh was right.

Now I see that sadness is sticking to me. Sometimes I am so sad that crying doesn't even help me. In Iran, whenever I felt depressed, I cried and felt relief. But now, even if I were to cry every day and every night, nothing would change.

Last night, I sat by the window until it was dark. I couldn't see the snow any more, but I knew it was still snowing. Marzieh came home late. She had to work overtime. I was feeling down. It was time to do the night prayer. Whenever I pray, Marzieh makes fun of me and says, "Maman, the God here isn't the same as your God over there. Here, God can't understand Arabic, you should talk to Him in English."

"That's blasphemy," I say. "There's only one God. Wherever you go, He's the same. He understands all languages. God rescued you and made me cry and fool the guards, when ordinarily I'm not the kind of person to cry and ask for anything. In the years since your father died, I raised you by sewing and knitting. Have you ever seen me ask anybody for anything? That day, what I did was just for you. If I had done nothing, they would have not only searched my house, perhaps they would have looked for you in the neighbours' houses too. God rescued you. If anything happened to you, I couldn't go on living."

My poor son Ahmad lost his life for nothing. How I miss his young wife and his baby. I wish I could send them some of this milk powder, or some of this baby food. But I don't have any money. Marzieh goes to work at seven o'clock in the morning and comes back at seven in the evening. When she comes back, she is like a dead person. Most of the money she earns is paid for rent. I've never seen our landlord. I really don't know if there is one. Anyway, we pay the rent. Who gets it? God only knows. Marzieh receives money in one hand and gives it away in the other. What does Marzieh get? Nothing, just fatigue. She's getting older. I feel sorry for her. It's amazing how much a person can stand. After my poor Ahmad was killed in the war I missed him so much. He sacrificed himself for nothing. I told him several times that he shouldn't go to the front. But he said, "I have to go."

They took him away from his workplace to go to war. He didn't last two months. His poor baby never saw her father. So many sorrows to choose from. It's amazing how much a person can bear. But this homesickness is worst of all.

All day, I sit by the window. I knit, I read the Koran, but what use are they? Last night I was so depressed. Marzieh came home late. She wasn't in a good mood either. She didn't even speak to me.

"What's the matter?" I asked.

She said nothing.

"What?" I said. "You look sad."

"Don't ask," she said. "I'm so frustrated here."

"Don't say that, Marzieh," I said. "You are very lucky to be here."

"No, I'm not. I would like to go back." She said, "I'm a stranger here, and I always will be a stranger."

"You can't go back home," I said. "Don't even think about it."

I saw the tears in her eyes. She went to her room and closed the door.

I knew she had gone to her room to cry. I was depressed too. Since the day I came to this land, I've felt down. A piece of stone is lying on my heart. It's hard for me to breathe. But I have to be hopeful. Last night when Marzieh was so sad, I saw tears in her eyes, and when she locked herself in her room, I felt a sharp blade tearing my heart. I turned the light off, and tears really began to flow. I thought of snow, falling like my tears, without stop. I wondered, what if Marzieh came out of her room and asked why am I crying? What would I answer? But I couldn't help it. Tears wouldn't stop pouring; a flooded river isn't easy to stop. I put my head under the quilt to smother my sobs. Suddenly I remembered God. The God who rescued my Marzieh. The one who taught me how to cry and scream to rescue Marzieh. I called God, God…I don't know how many times I called Him. Maybe a thousand, ten thousand, a hundred thousand, I don't know. I cried and called God. I was sure He would hear me. It seemed that someone was telling me that if I call God, He will answer me. I called Him and asked Him, "Take me back to my home, the place where I belong. Marzieh and me. I don't want to stay in this land. I don't want the meat, the fruit and the beautiful dresses. I don't want to go shopping in those big stores. Take me back to Sayed Taghi street, now called Martyr Rahmani. I promise I'll wait in line every morning for milk and meat rations, and even bread. I can get along with just bread and yogurt. Just take me to my home; Marzieh and me. I know that Hamid is waiting for her. I know he is not released yet, but he is waiting for her. I hope that the revolutionary guards have forgotten about Marzieh. I will change her name."

I called out to God, "If you take Marzieh and me back and no one hurts Marzieh I will be your slave for the rest of my life. I will pray ten times a day. I will fast for two months every year. I will be your true slave."

Talking to God, I muffled my sobs under the quilt. I fell

asleep calling God. When I opened my eyes, I saw Marzieh sitting by my bed. She looked at me and said,

"What's the matter? Are you sick?"

"No," I said.

"Yes, you are," she said. "You look pale, and your eyes are red."

I started to cry again.

"What happened?" she said. "Tell me."

"Last night I asked God all night to take us back to our home," I said.

Marzieh laughed and asked, "Well, what did He answer?"

"Nothing," I said. "He didn't answer me."

"Let Him be," She said. "Don't ask Him anymore."

"You're right," I said. "The God here isn't ours."

"No," she said, "There's no God anywhere for us."

Interview

With my face
          colourless
and hers painted
          colourful
I was nothing
          — blank.

I looked at her —
          destitute
she smiled at me
          — inane.

I left the room
hope melting in
          my hands.

She wished me
          good luck
I wished her
          death

Such a nice
          woman!
I hate her.

~ In Limbo ~

It was one of those beautiful days. The sky was blue and inviting, soothing and kind. Blue so clear it took your mind off work just to look at it. A pleasing blue sky which flows through you, connects your very existence with the sky, the trees, with the earth and nature. That day the sky was truly beautiful. The weather was friendly, like an invitation to live. You could feel it with all your being.

Nargess looked at the sky. She tried to ignore it. Spring should not evoke these feelings in her. She didn't have time for them. She had to be completely focused on her work.

When Margaret came in, Nargess looked up from her monitor and said, "Good morning."

"Good morning," Margaret replied smiling, then, looking at the sky added, "Great weather." There was sincerity in her blue eyes. Nargess, as usual, had started work early. Margaret commented, "Early bird."

Nargess smiled. She always smiled in response. Words were not friendly to her. The sentences she spoke, the sentences she heard — she was always struggling with them. She wanted to say so much, but she was unable to frame her thoughts. She lacked the words. She thought, "I don't need the words. I convey my ideas without talking." She felt Margaret could understand her.

With a cup of coffee in her hand, Margaret came and asked, "Don't you drink coffee?"

"No, I don't like it. It bothers my stomach," Nargess responded.

"Why don't you take a break? You deserve it."

"Okay, I'll come," Nargess agreed. But when they went to the other room and sat on the sofa, Nargess felt uncomfortable. She didn't know why. She couldn't speak, although there were many things to say. She urgently needed to talk, but she didn't have the language. If only the words were not so strange to her.

Diana and Clair were chattering. Nargess ignored them. Listening required concentration, and she didn't have it. Margaret said, "You look tired. Why? Have you heard from your husband?" Nargess was looking down and then looked up into Margaret's eyes. Why was she so far away from her? Like the sky. With all her kindness, so far away.

Nargess responded, "Oh, yes, I have." Joy radiated in Margaret's blue eyes. She no longer wanted to know why Nargess was upset, why she looked down. Nargess would have liked to talk to Margaret. She wanted to tell her about her problems. She wanted to tell her that her husband was not the only person she was worried about. To tell her there were also her brother and sister, her friends, many friends back in her homeland. "There" was her country, her home. All of her memories, and part of her being, were back there. She wanted to say that she could never be complete without them, but her English wasn't adequate. How could she explain all this, using the few words she knew! Instead, she stayed silent. Nargess looked at Margaret's eyes, blue as the sky, gentle and sincere, but far away, very far away.

After the break, she went to her desk, looked at the sky, still a clear blue. It brought tears to her eyes. She wondered if they would fire her. She wished she could talk to Margaret about it. But something was blocking her — pride, shame or lack of language?

Her English was just not enough to speak clearly. Her sentences were vague. She always wondered if people understood her, understood what she really meant. Her communication with them seemed always one-sided and uncertain, as if a curtain separated her from others. She never spoke more than three or four sentences at a time, and even those sentences were incomplete. That was why she was always upset and quiet. She had two eyes to watch and two ears to hear. She listened but couldn't hear. Words couldn't reach her. There was a barrier between them. When she couldn't understand what people said, a fog would come over her, and she would sink deeper and deeper into it.

Nargess thought to herself, "Margaret thinks my only problem is my husband. She thinks I have no other problems. Ah, I wish I could talk with her." She wondered, "What does she think of me? Does she think I'm stupid? A wandering, homeless person? Poor, weak, needy and desperate?" Nargess hated herself. She felt that she hated Margaret too. She looked at the sky which was still so blue. Then Nargess looked at the monitor.

Figures were flying around. She had made so many mistakes that day. She made mistakes all the time. Margaret looked over at Nargess' work and became quiet. There was a thought in her blue eyes. Nargess thought, "She's not kind any more. I screwed up again. Maybe it's because of the sky. I wish I were sitting under a tree. I wish I had no problems." She was upset. How many problems she had! Which one should she be thinking about — if her son failed his exam, how could she afford his expenses? What if her husband were to get killed in an Iraqi missile attack on Tehran?

A bittersweet smile appeared on her face when she thought, "My husband... doesn't he have a name?" Speaking to Margaret, she had always referred to "Bahram" as "My husband," and now, she was becoming accustomed to not using his name. Was she going to forget it altogether, and her son's as well? Those names were unfamiliar to Margaret. Just the day before Margaret had shown her an Iranian name, asking for its proper pronunciation. "Nasser." Margaret had repeated "Nazer." The name was strange to Margaret, but to Nargess it was her younger brother. Where was he? She didn't know.

Nargess knew he had escaped from Iran, but she didn't have any idea where he would be now — Pakistan, India, Sweden? Nobody knew. They had been scattered all over the world. Bahram had informed her that her house in Iran was about to be sold. So, she didn't have a home any more. She had nothing.

Nargess really needed to talk to Margaret, to talk to someone to relieve herself a little of these burdens. Talking to Iranians was fruitless; they had their own problems. Margaret was enjoying life. The joy of life was in her blue eyes. Nargess wanted to talk to her about her anguish. Perhaps Margaret would comfort her. Margaret was deep like the sea. She would accept her. But Nargess kept silent. She just talked to herself. Margaret was sitting next to her, trying to help her with work.

Margaret was talking now. "Listen, if you work like this, they won't like you. They won't accept you. They are not easygoing people. A maximum of two errors a day is acceptable, no more than that."

Nargess' hands turned cold. It's over. They would fire her.

One more misery on top of all the other miseries. She wanted to say, "I try, I do my best. I'm able to learn. I'm not stupid. This is not difficult. In Iran, my work was much more difficult. I could do it without mistakes. Please give me some more time. Be moderate."

"Moderate!" The word made her laugh. How did that word come into her mind? She really couldn't put it into English. She'd have to find some other word. *Modara* was such a nice word. But it didn't apply to the situation. She had never used it before.

She suddenly thought, "I'll write her a letter, I'll try to explain my situation. My problems." But for whom? For what? It wasn't one person's decision. And Margaret didn't have any influence. It was the system. Work is the only thing that is of value. You have to know how to do it without errors. Nargess wished she was able to put her thoughts and her imagination into her purse and close it tightly. She thought about the screen and her fingers hitting the wrong keys. She hated the mistakes. She didn't see them most of the time, Margaret did. She caught them. They were everywhere, hidden, and the next minute they just appeared. She felt hot. She wanted to kick the computer, but Margaret was sitting right beside her.

Margaret showed her the mistakes and Nargess went red. She was sweating and tired. She was so tired. That day, she just kept on making mistakes. Margaret remarked on all of them. But she had looked at her gently and said, "You look tired." Nargess had wanted to say, "Right, I am tired, tired enough to die." But she didn't. It was no use.

She just wished she had a computer in her head instead of her brain. It would be good if she didn't have feelings, didn't have thoughts. A hollow head, filled with a calculator.

She thought her head was empty, really empty. Sorrow occupied her head, occupied every single cell of her body.

The sky was still blue when she got out of the office. Clouds were accumulating along the horizon. Nargess thought, "What would I ever do if Margaret wasn't here? So many mistakes."

But then, outside under that glorious, soothing blue sky, Nargess grew calm. She became inspired. "I'll do better tomorrow! I'll do my best. I'll even be careful, as if I had four eyes." Words were strange to her. Whenever she would say anything she first had to look for the words, and then they would escape her. Nargess thought, "I'll try. I have to make it." Then she looked at the sky again. It looked nicer, more beautiful. The blue sky always consoled her.

for Mary Thornbury

Roots

Your memories — remote
your children — alien
your future — vague
looking for the past
buried in other
                    land!

Your words
in your hands — strange
your identity — a NUMBER
hard to remember

Spring without birds
trees without roots.

BUT your faith in rebirth
                is your nest.

~ Newcomer ~

The class had already started when Sussan came in. She found a seat in the last row and sat down. The teacher said something, but Sussan did not understand. She just smiled. Sussan had come up the stairs fast, her heart was beating like a drum. The teacher was talking to the students. Sussan couldn't understand. She had been coming to this ESL class for two months. The words still had a strange sound to her. She had learned "Hello," "Goodbye," "Yes" and "No." She had no problem using the first two. She knew where to use them but she always had problem with "Yes" and "No." She misused them; answering questions sometimes she would say "yes" and after seeing the reaction of the other person, she would say "no."

The teacher was talking about the past tense. Sussan sometimes understood the meaning of the sentences. The teacher wrote, "I had a house." The sentence stuck in her mind. She had a house too. She had a past too. She lost her concentration and dreamily went back to her own house.

The teacher wrote, "My house was big." Sussan's reading was better than her listening. Her house was big too. Masoud had built a one-floor building on the big plot of land they had inherited from her father. The building was surrounded by tall trees. She could see them through the window. There was white poplar and fruit trees. They were full of blossoms in the spring and in the summer they encircled the house as if it was a baby.

The teacher wrote, "I liked my house." Sussan thought about the big living room with windows on two sides, about the Tabriz rug like a painting, full of flowers and animals. She thought about the big ceramic bowl inherited from her grandfather, about when Nima broke it with a ball and she had punished Nima and he had cried. The keepsake from her grandfather was chipped.

Sussan thought about Nima. He was eighteen when the revolution started in Iran, and... The teacher noticed her, and asked "What is it?" Then she asked a question, a long one. Sussan did not understand, but tried to smile. She tried to wipe out Nima's memory, along with that of her house and the ceramic bowl. The teacher and other students were looking at her. A girl from India sat in front of her. She had braided hair and a tanned face. She wore a *sari* under her pink coat. Her green georgette *sari* reminded Sussan of Indian movies. The girl turned back and stared at Sussan. Sussan just smiled. Her smile was her only means of communication.

The teacher left Sussan alone. Sussan looked at the blackboard. The teacher had covered it with words that Sussan more or less knew. A Vietnamese man who sat at the front desk, raised his hand and asked something. The teacher repeated his question. Sussan understood the teacher better than she understood the other students. Sussan didn't hear some of the man's question and what she did hear was incomprehensible to her. She just guessed the meaning of the rest. Apparently he had said something about his country. She thought he had said, "My country was big." Sussan told herself, "My country was big too." If she had had the courage, she would have said this sentence out loud. But she was afraid. She was unable to say it. Instead, she silently dreamt about her country, about the winding roads, about the mountains, about the cities she had visited, about the trip they had taken to the city of Shiraz. She had driven half of the way and Masoud the other half. Nima, Kaveh and Mozhgan had sat in the back seat. Sometimes they sang, sometimes they slept, sometimes they argued over something. She stared at the roads, the trees, the valleys and the newly-harvested land. How much she loved travelling around the country.

Valentina raised her hand. Valentina was from South America. She was the only person whose name Sussan had learned. Valentina reminded her of her sister, Simin. It was three months since Sussan had left Iran and they had not heard anything about her. She did not know if Rozbeh was back from the war front. She had received a letter from her brother Saeed, but he hadn't mentioned him. When Sussan told Masoud, "I don't know why he has not written about Rozbeh," Masoud had replied, "He must have forgotten. You know your brother and how absent-minded he is. What do you expect from him?" Valentina was still talking to the teacher. Sussan listened. She tried to pay attention, she dismissed Simin from her mind and listened to Valentina.

Valentina was talking with difficulty. The words would not come to her mouth. She seemed to need time to find a word. She lost the words in her mind and was looking for replacements. Sussan thought, "She is like me. I also have to think a lot before I say something. I even forget the few words I know or else I misuse them." Valentina was talking about revolution. Sussan knew this word very well. But she was not able to pronounce it. It was a difficult word, and her tongue couldn't twist around it. Sussan thought, "I wish that all people would talk the same language." She wanted to understand all that Valentina said. She wished that she could talk about the revolution. She wished she could understand the revolution. She wanted to know why there was a revolution in her country and why the revolution took her son away from her. Why the revolution forced her to sell the house she had inherited from her grandfather and why her family had to risk death to pass through the mountains, to flee from her country.

The teacher was talking to Valentina. Valentina had to spend a lot of time on every sentence. The teacher was very patient. Sussan couldn't understand what they were saying. She had a lot of questions in her mind.

On the other side of the classroom, a young man whom Sussan did not know got into the conversation. Then a third person joined in. It was clear that revolution was an interesting subject. The whole class was talking about it. Sussan was the only person who was quiet.

The teacher asked her something. Sussan thought the teacher was asking for her opinion. She went red. She did not know what to say. What if she said "yes" and it did not make sense. So it was better to say "no." When the teacher heard "no" she smiled. The whole class laughed. Sussan went even redder. She felt the sweat break out on her forehead. Then she smiled at the teacher. But she felt a bitter sorrow. She wished she could talk about the revolution, about the day when the three guards had come to her home. They had rummaged through the entire house. They had looked through her photo album and made fun of it. She wanted to tell everyone about those days when the guards would not let them water the flowers and they had died in the June sunshine, about the days the whole family was in jail, even twelve-year-old Mozhgan. Two weeks later when they were released, Nima was no longer with them. Nima had been executed, two nights after being arrested.

Sussan wished she could talk, but there was a piece of wood in her mouth instead of her tongue, a lump in her throat. She turned her eyes away from blackboard and looked at the floor to hide her tears. The whole class was talking. Words were vague sounds playing with her thoughts and memories. And she could not understand anything. She was quiet.

The class finished. But the real silence was within her. She looked at the papers the teacher handed her. She knew all the letters but most of the words had no meaning for her. A pain of humiliation gripped her heart. She thought. "I must learn. I have to learn. I cannot stay silent..."

~ Without Root ~

Mother says it's all my fault.

But, I don't agree. Everyone likes to put the blame on somebody else. Well, I do. Maybe I'm wrong, but if Mother and Father put themselves in my place and were fair, they would see I'm not. They think it's easy for us to adjust to a new society and culture. Father, especially, always talks about his roots in Iran, says he is going to die here like a plant without roots.

What about us children? How can we have roots here? If we stay locked inside our homes, we'll never put down roots anywhere! And even if we do, they won't be firm. Father doesn't want to understand, and doesn't want to think about it. He and Mother are stuck in their Iranian culture and customs. "We have to preserve."

No one is going to ask them, "When you were planning to escape from Iran, why didn't you think about these things then?"

Father's reasons are clear and in his opinion, very sound. Firstly, it was on account of Behzad and me. Secondly, for himself — when his career ended. He was a colonel in the Iranian army and was afraid that if he appeared to be against the revolution, his property would be taken by the government.

Well, he had no choice but to leave the country. Or, as

115

he says, "I had to." For two years he couldn't find a job here. He didn't want to learn English. He went to ESL classes reluctantly and found out how hard it is to learn. He left after one year.

Poor Mother was working day and night in a donut shop in those days. Father's nerves were in such a state we always had to keep voices low at home. He hated Behzad's long hair. One day he grabbed the scissors and cut it. We laughed at him — how funny it looked. Then Mother cut it again, properly, all the while cursing and groaning. At first she couldn't do hairdressing. Now she's an expert. The haircuts she gives me are so beautiful, no one believes me when I say that my mother did it.

I suggested to her, "Open a hairdressing business."

"Who will come?" she asked. "And if they do, won't they expect me to do it for free?" She didn't go into business, she does her friends' hair for free.

When Father is angry he always says, "In a foreign land, if you close one eye, the other one won't give up its light. Why are you devoting your free time to others?" But he is just like her. When Mrs. Soraya was moving, he lent her his cab for the day and switched to the night shift. Mother was angry and thought that there was something between them. Poor Mrs. Soraya. Her husband was an army officer executed during the revolution, leaving her with two small children. Father respects her and says, "She is the only woman who has not changed here. Most are no longer themselves. They take one whiff of freedom and become unbridled." My father talks about women as if they are sheep. Whenever Mother says something, he sneers at her, and then laughs. This makes Mother very angry.

Once when he ridiculed me, I cursed him with dirty words in English. Lucky for me that he didn't understand.

Behzad giggled. Mother didn't understand either. Father screamed, "What did she say?" Mother looked innocent and said, "How do I know? I haven't grown up in Canada."

But Behzad continued laughing. Father finally understood that I'd cursed him. If we'd been in Iran, and I said such things, he would have punished me, sent me to the basement, and perhaps hit me too. Who would have dared say anything rude to my father over there? When he became a colonel, he would stand in front of the mirror in his uniform and ask Mother, "Ashraf, how is this?" And Mother had to admire him and smooth any wrinkles from the shoulders of his jacket.

Father would sometimes talk about the soldiers and officers under his command. He would send for his army servant at home and scold him for no reason. I didn't know what was going on. I remember going to Aunt Nasrin's house and Father would make fun of her husband. He'd say, "Yoosef is his wife's servant. He serves the guests, he does the dishes." He especially targeted Yoosef's dishwashing. At home Father never lifted a finger. Aunt Nasrin thought Mother was lucky having a servant.

I sometimes wish Aunt Nasrin was here to see Father wash the dishes. When Mother was working and he was staying at home. And, especially the time Mother was in hospital with appendicitis.

I would come home late on purpose and mumble an excuse. "I had...class." Mother blamed me for Father having to wash dishes. Mother seemed to think that Father belonged to a special species whose masculinity would be lost if he washed some dishes. Since he began working as a taxi driver, he has touched nothing at home. If he came home and found Mother out, if she'd gone shopping, for example, he'd blame me. But I didn't care about him. I heard what he said with one ear and it went right out the other. He thought I was like her, that he could bully me.

One day when he grabbed my ear, I warned him, "You be careful, or I'll call the Children's Aid."

His eyes opened wide, "What did you say?"

Behzad was laughing, but controlled himself when he saw Father about to slap him. Behzad seized his hand, "You know what Children's Aid means?"

Father was stupefied. "What does it mean?"

"If she calls and tells them you hit her," Behzad replied coldly, "they will come and take her away and give her to a family who does a better job with her."

Father was about to slap Behzad again, but suddenly he sat down, put his head between his hands and sobbed like a child. Mother came in and asked, "What happened?"

He shouted at her. Behzad continued, "Father, Mother can complain about you too. So stop shouting so loudly!" Then Behzad said that wife assault is a criminal offence here, but I'm sure neither of them believed him. Father was cross for a few days. He didn't talk to any of us. Mother had to treat him gently. She grumbled at Behzad and me, "Why were you bothering him?"

We told her, "Father should change his behaviour."

She didn't agree, "Poor man! In Iran he was such a remarkable person, an army unit under his command. If they saw his shadow, they wouldn't dare breathe — they might be slapped or spat upon. Now his children curse him."

"Here it's different," Behzad said. "I mean everybody has value, even the animals are protected."

Mother didn't want to listen to us. "That has nothing to do with us," she replied. "We have our own culture and our own traditions. In our culture, children must obey their parents. They should respect their elders. They should not complain when they are hit or punished."

Mother never stopped giving advice. If Father was in a good mood, he would join in with his favourite poems and proverbs. He would recite them for us in order to hammer Iranian culture into our heads. The longer we live in Canada, the more Mother and Father mention the value of Iranian culture and Iranian tradition. At first they ignored *Chelleh* night and *Noruz*. Later on, however, for *Chelleh* night Mother invited friends in and served the watermelon and pomegranate which father had searched for all over the city. Mother also cooked her own special *Fesenjan*, and *Ghorme sabzi*. Father told fortunes, using Hafez's poetry, reading the poems aloud. When we asked, "What does it mean?" he wouldn't answer exactly. Just that it was good or it was bad. Then he wanted us to tell him what our wishes were. I didn't wish for anything.

When we arrived Father was only interested in assimilating quickly into Canadian society. He used to tell us to make friends with Canadian children. I brought Salima home with me one time. After she left, Father and Mother made fun of her and said, "Why do you make friends with coloured children?"

Father sneered, "The pot always looks for its own lid."

I asked, "What does that mean?" His explanation was meant to show me that I'm coloured too.

When I was older, kids would ask, "Are you Hindu or Pakistani?" I answered, "I'm Irani."

"Where is Iran?" they would ask. I wished Father and Mother could have heard those questions, so they wouldn't force us to be proud of our country. Maybe one day we will be proud of our homeland, but first we have to know who we are.

In those early days, Father used to say, "If you don't want people to look at you, you'd better blend in." I was so young then — just ten. Behazad was thirteen. Father wanted us to learn English and make Canadian friends. After a few years he found out that for him to be Canadian was not easy to do. But it was for us. We spoke English without an accent, and if we didn't have black hair it would have been hard to tell that we had only been in Canada five years. But for Mother and Father it was different. They stayed home more and socialized with Iranian friends. As our time in Canada grew longer, they tried to discourage us from making friends with our Canadian classmates. "You won't be nice anymore," Mother used to say.

The day Behzad pierced his ear, Father almost brought the house down. But he didn't dare hit him. I'm sure he was afraid of the Children's Aid. He threatened to throw himself over the balcony. An Irani man of the same age had killed himself about the same time. I didn't take his threats seriously. In my view they were just to frighten us. But poor Mother was always anxious. Sometimes she fainted or grabbed her hair and pulled it.

Another time when Behzad shouted at Father, "Why are you bothering us so much?" Father cried. What a mess. Behzad said to father, "I spit on that army you commanded." Father stared at him, wanting to hit him. Mother led him away to the bedroom and gave him a glass of cold beer. Things were calm for a couple of weeks. Behzad removed his earring and cut his hair. But one day I saw him in the street on the way to school and he was wearing an earring. He said he only put it away at home.

I pierced my right ear a second time. I'm lucky that my hair is long and covers my ears. Otherwise there would have been another row at home.

Mrs. Shokri, who comes to school sometimes to help Iranian students, told my parents about Allen. I don't know how she found out about us. I'm sixteen years old, in Grade Eleven, and didn't have a boyfriend till now. In fact, kids teased me, and called me "Virginia." I can't believe they all sleep with their boyfriends — most of them are Pakistani, Hindu or Chinese, with their own cultures, traditions. At least their parents have strong beliefs. I didn't know why they made fun of me! I was scared to have a boyfriend. Mother always used to tell me, "You should keep your virginity. You should be such and such, for your first night of your marriage. No man should touch you before marriage."

She used to tell me many things about boys, and I believed them. That to have a boyfriend would happen naturally. I tried to be the girl Mother would like me to be. But it didn't work. First, because the kids teased me. Secondly, I liked Allen. He was tall and blond. He was the most handsome boy in our class. When Salima heard that Allen and I were friends, she almost died of jealousy. She knew how my parents thought. I mean, I had talked to her about everything. She was crazy about Allen. I went home from school with him, but I didn't sleep with him. He never mentioned this. We were just friends.

When Father and Mother found out about us they made my life miserable. Father hit me hard. I wanted to call the

Children's Aid, but didn't. In fact, I felt sorry for them, especially for Mother. She was always crying as if I had died. Father said, "It would be better for us to go back to Iran. Even if they arrest me and put me in jail, it will be better than here."

Mother objected, "We can't go. Don't you know how expensive life is over there? We have nothing left. We spent all the money we had." Mother's reasons convinced Father.

The day he saw me with Allen in the street there was another big scene. It was Allen's fault, he hugged me and kissed me just as Father's cab passed by. I turned and saw him stop. He stopped in the middle of street. I was sure he had seen me. That night he didn't come home. Mother came to my room very upset. Behzad was studying in the living room. He was in his first year of university and had to work hard. We all felt anxious. Mother called Father's workplace. They said they hadn't heard from him since afternoon.

We didn't hear from Father for a week. Mother called everywhere he was supposed to be, even the airport, but couldn't find out anything. Then he called home. Mother came back to life. "Where are you calling from?" she asked.

Behzad and I were listening as Mother talked. When she finished her telephone conversation, she smiled and said, "He's nearby, he'll be coming home soon."

Now, months later, some nights he still calls her. When she puts down the receiver, she always says, "He's going to come back home, soon."

Chelleh night — *the first night of the winter, also the longest night of the year, and is celebrated by Iranians.*
Noruz — *Iranian new year*
Fesenjan and Ghorme sabzi — *traditional Iranian foods*

Photo: Arash Mohtashami

Mehri Yalfani was born in Hamadan, Iran. After high school, she moved to Tehran to pursue her education in engineering at the University of Tehran. She graduated in 1963 with a degree in electrical engineering and worked as an engineer for twenty years in government administration and at the Tehran Cement Plant. Mehri Yalfani began to write when she was in high school. Her first short story collection was published in 1966 and a novel, *Before the Fall*, in 1980, both in Iran. In 1987 Mehri Yalfani immigrated to Canada and has since published many short stories in Iranian publications as well as a short story collection, *Birthday Party*, in 1991 and a second novel, *Someone is Coming*, in Sweden in 1994. She writes in Farsi, her mother language and wishes one day to translate all her work into English. Mehri is currently working on a novel, *Far From Home*. *Parastoo* is her first English-language book.